Praise for

SCARLET and IVY

"This is one of the best books I have ever read. It was exciting, funny, warm and mysterious." **Lily, aged 9**

"The whole book was brilliant... after the first paragraph it was as though Ivy was my best friend." **Ciara, aged 10**

"This book is full of excitement and adventure – a masterpiece!" **Jennifer, aged 9**

"This is a page-turning mystery adventure with puzzles that keep you guessing." **Felicity, aged 11**

"A brilliant and exciting book." **Evie, aged 8**

"The story shone with excitement, secrets and bonds of friendship... If I had to mark this book out of 10, I would give it 11!" **Sidney, aged 11**

SOPHIE CLEVERLY was born in Bath in 1989. She wrote her first story at the age of four, though it used no punctuation and was essentially one long sentence. Thankfully, things have improved somewhat since then, and she has earned a BA in Creative Writing and an MA in Writing for Young People from Bath Spa University.

Now working as a full-time writer, Sophie lives with her husband in Wiltshire, where she has a house full of books and a garden full of crows.

Books by Sophie Cleverly

The Scarlet and Ivy series
in reading order

THE LOST TWIN

THE WHISPERS IN THE WALLS

THE DANCE IN THE DARK

THE LIGHTS UNDER THE LAKE

SCARLET and IVY

The Lights Under the Lake

SOPHIE CLEVERLY

HarperCollins *Children's Books*

First published in Great Britain by
HarperCollins *Children's Books* in 2017
HarperCollins *Children's Books* is a division of HarperCollins*Publishers* Ltd,
HarperCollins Publishers
1 London Bridge Street
London SE1 9GF

www.harpercollins.co.uk
2

ISBN 978–0–00–821833–1

Typeset in Lido/11pt by Palimpsest Book Production Ltd, Falkirk, Stirlingshire
Printed and bound in Great Britain by Clays Ltd, St Ives plc

MIX
Paper from
responsible sources
FSC C007454

For Lizzie – thank you for believing in Scarlet and Ivy

Chapter One

IVY

Scarlet and I were a team that couldn't be broken. She was my twin; my reflection in the mirror; the other side of the same coin. As long as we were together, there was nothing we couldn't face. That was what we'd promised each other. We could do anything.

But this wasn't *quite* what I'd had in mind.

"Hold still!" yelled Ariadne. "Just one more minute!"

I looked at Scarlet in horror. By my estimation, we had less than a minute before Miss Bowler arrived and we were all in hideous trouble, and about ten seconds before I lost my balance and plunged straight into the water.

Scarlet was staring back at me, the expression frozen on her face. "I hate you, Ariadne," she said, twisting her mouth without moving her eyes.

Ariadne had received a camera from her father as a present during the Easter holidays, and it was her new obsession. It was small, black and silver, with knobs and dials that clicked and whirred. And right at that moment we were being subjected to it.

"It's going to look *magical*!" she shouted from the other side of the pool.

I was wobbling. I tried very hard not to think about the chilly water just inches from my toes, and even harder not to think about what I was wearing.

This was Ariadne's brilliant idea: Scarlet and I were to dress as water nymphs and pose on the diving boards of Rookwood School's horrible outdoor pool. She had made us costumes out of old swimsuits and ballet tutus, with streamers of blue and green, and chalked streaks of colour on our faces. She'd scattered flowers in the water around us. I was certain that we looked quite ridiculous.

She wanted us both to do an *arabesque*, the ballet move where you stand on tiptoe with your arms outstretched and one leg up behind you, in a mirror image of each other. And now she was on the far side of the pool, bobbing up and down with the camera as she tried to get the perfect angle.

"Who agreed to this, again?" I whispered to Scarlet.

The diving boards were cold and slippery, even in the morning sun. Lessons were about to start, and Miss Bowler was *not* going to be happy if her first swimming session of the day was disrupted by two failed water nymphs tumbling into the deep end.

"Ariadneeee!" Scarlet wailed as her leg started to give.

"There. Got it!" Ariadne exclaimed finally. "You can stop now!"

"Oh, thank goodness," I said, lowering my raised leg gently to the ground and slowly backing off the board. I could feel my muscles twitching. Scarlet just sat down with a thump, making her board thrum with vibrations.

Our best friend wandered over to us. She was clutching her camera and grinning, seemingly oblivious to our close brush with peril. "I think this will be my best photograph yet. Daddy will be so pleased." She'd been learning how to develop her pictures in the new darkroom and sending them to her father in the post. Apparently he was proudly displaying them on the walls of Flitworth Manor.

"Never make me do that again," said Scarlet. Ariadne just blinked at her happily.

"GIRLS!" came a sudden booming voice.

"Uh-oh." The colour drained from our friend's face.

The huge figure of Miss Bowler came striding past the changing rooms towards us, her whistle swinging back and forth round her neck. "What do you think you're doing? Is this some sort of *art*?" She bellowed the word as if it were something terrible and offensive.

"I... um..." Ariadne stammered, holding the camera out in front of herself as if it would protect her.

Miss Bowler glared at us furiously. "You should all be in lessons. My class is about to start and the pool is full of GREENERY!"

"I'll clear it up, Miss!" Ariadne squeaked. She ran and grabbed a net that was leaning against the wall and began trying to sweep the flowers from the water. The camera bounced on its leather strap as she moved.

The swimming instructor turned her glare to my twin. "I expect better from you, Ivy."

"I'm Scarlet," said Scarlet.

Miss Bowler went red. "I don't care who you are! Clean up this mess and get inside! And for goodness' sake, put your uniforms back on!"

I looked down at myself sheepishly. Ariadne had made a brave effort with her costumes, and she was certainly a good seamstress, but she wasn't exactly at the level of our Aunt Sara.

I hoped Miss Bowler had finished her shouting, but evidently she hadn't. "Flitworth, if I see you messing around with that infernal gadget during lesson time again, I will take it off you! Do you understand?"

Ariadne dropped a sopping pile of flowers at her feet. "Yes, Miss! I'll put it away, Miss!"

Miss Bowler's face contorted with disgust. "Children," she muttered with distaste. "I've a good mind to make you swim la—" She cut herself off, and looked over her shoulder, some of the tomato red draining from her cheeks. I wondered if she was remembering our new headmistress Mrs Knight's aversion to punishments, or perhaps old Headmaster Bartholomew and the girl who had once drowned at his hands in the school lake. Either way, she seemed to change her mind. "Just get inside," she said finally, before stomping away.

I looked back at Ariadne, expecting her to be upset. She loved that camera, and hated being told off. But her worried expression had changed to an excited grin. She waved the camera at us. "I can't wait to see how this one turns out!"

Rookwood School was trying its best to return to normality. Or at least, what passed for normality at a place where there really was at least one actual skeleton in the cupboard.

Last term, girls had left the school in droves, their parents afraid it was unsafe. And they were right, it turned out – our terrifying headmistress Miss Fox had stopped at nothing in trying to destroy the reputation of Rookwood School, but we'd finally thwarted her.

So Rookwood was a safe place once again, but that didn't mean everyone had come back. Some had enrolled at other schools for good, their parents horrified by the spate of poisonings and anonymous threats. Violet, former arch-enemy of Scarlet, had been taken away by her guardian, and nobody had heard from her since. Not even Rose, who Violet had rescued from the asylum and brought to Rookwood. Rose had been allowed to stay while efforts were made to find out where she came from.

Things were now as normal as they could be. Lessons, porridge and stew, detentions for Scarlet; all under the now slightly more watchful eye of Mrs Knight. And now, I supposed, under the lens of Ariadne's camera.

The next day began, as they tended to do, with an assembly.

We were shuffling into the hall when Mrs Knight breezed past us, clutching a piece of paper.

"Looks like an announcement," said Scarlet, craning her neck to see over the first formers.

"Oooh," said Ariadne. "I hope it's a good one. Perhaps they're going to improve the school dinners." I was amazed that she had managed to keep up her appetite after being poisoned by the stew last term.

"Maybe they're cancelling all the lessons. Or firing all the teachers and letting us run the school," my twin suggested, her face suddenly hopeful.

I laughed and took a seat in our row, praying the announcement would actually be about something good, and not another one of the 'unfortunate incidents' that Rookwood was becoming famous for.

But as Mrs Knight took to the stage, I could see a twinkle of excitement in her eyes. "Good morning, girls," she called cheerfully.

"Good morning, Mrs Knight," we chorused back. The chorus wasn't quite as loud as it had been before we'd lost so many students.

"Before we go on to the hymns this morning, I have an announcement to make!" she said. "And I think this is one you'll all enjoy."

Scarlet nudged me. "*Firing all the teachers*," she mouthed.

"We could all do with a fresh start after last term," Mrs Knight continued. I felt that was a bit of an understatement. "And so I have prepared a special treat: a school trip!"

A ripple of excited murmurs spread across the hall. Mrs Knight held out her hands to quieten everyone down, looking unusually pleased with herself.

"Now, girls, this will be a great opportunity to show some Rookwood School spirit. We will be staying at a wonderful lakeside hotel for a week of nature activities and working together."

Scarlet and Ariadne were grinning, but I felt a tiny shiver down my spine. I wasn't sure I wanted to go near another lake.

"Parents have already been notified by letter so they can give permission and pay the fees." She smiled down at her notes. "There will also be a notice in the local paper. We want to show just how great our school can be."

Hmm. I could see what she was up to. She was putting her brave face back on, and hoping that this would rescue the school's reputation. I wasn't sure it would be enough. The murderous and swindling headteachers of the past had done too much damage, surely?

Miss Bowler strutted on to the stage. "I don't want any dilly-dallyers on this trip, so you need to sign up on the sheet, or you won't be getting a place!"

Already everyone was whispering to each other in excitement. "We have to go," Scarlet said in my ear. "A whole week away from Rookwood! No lessons!"

"It sounds good," I muttered back.

"Oh, I do hope Daddy will let me go," said Ariadne.

I shuffled awkwardly in my seat. That was a point. If our

parents had to agree that we could go, *and* agree to pay the money… did we have any chance?

Mrs Knight continued: "Erm, right, yes, myself and Miss Bowler will be leading the trip, and there will be additional supervision from some of the elder prefects. Safety will be of the utmost importance, and we want everyone on their best behaviour."

My twin's expression was as mischievous as ever. "Easy," she whispered. "What could possibly go wrong?"

Chapter Two

SCARLET

As soon as the assembly was over, we ran for the sign-up sheet.

Or at least, *I* ran. And I might have shoved rather a lot of people out of the way. But what mattered was that I got there first, picked up the pen dangling from a string beside it, and wrote SCARLET GREY and IVY GREY in big letters on the top two lines and ARIADNE FLITWORTH just underneath.

"You can't write someone else's name," a girl behind me complained.

"I can," I said, pointing at the sheet. "I just did."

We *had* to go on this trip. There were no two ways about it. At last, an opportunity to get away from this horrible school for a whole week.

I stood back and watched as other girls began jostling to add their names to the list.

Ivy and Ariadne appeared next to me, having hurried to keep up.

"I added you both," I told them.

"Oh, goody!" said Ariadne, clapping excitedly. Ivy just looked a bit green.

"What's up with you, then, Ivy?" I asked.

"Do you think Father will agree to this?" she said after a pause. "Or more to the point, will Edith agree to it?"

She was right. Just having our names up there didn't mean anything if we couldn't get permission. I wasn't even sure if our father would be at home right now, or if he'd be off working in the big city somewhere, and that meant the person who would receive the letter would be Edith, our stepmother. I chewed my lip. This could be difficult.

"Ugh," I said. "You make a good point. I don't think she'd want to open her purse strings if we were starving on the streets, let alone to send us on a school trip."

Ivy nodded slowly. "We'll just have to wait and see, I suppose."

I looked back at the sheet – it was full already, and people were already trying to fit their names into the blank space round the side in the hopes that someone might drop out. Other notices had been knocked off the board and were scattered on the parquet floor of the entrance hall. I didn't think anything like this had ever happened at Rookwood before, at least not in recent years.

I clenched my fists, determined not to let our stepmother stop me.

"We're going," I said confidently. "And that's that."

"You're not going," Edith's voice sneered down the telephone, "and that's that."

We were sitting in Mrs Knight's office, just me and Ivy, and we'd been allowed to make a call. Apparently our dear stepmother had received the letter already, and wasn't impressed. "But why?" I whined. I knew I sounded childish, but I truly didn't understand. If it had been her precious boys, she would've said yes without a thought.

"Because it's a waste of my money, Scarlet," she snapped.

You mean Father's money, I thought, but I held my tongue for once. We stood no chance if I was rude to her. Even if she especially deserved it.

"I'm not paying for you to go off gallivanting about the

countryside when you should be learning," she continued. "Your father expects you to be getting a proper education, and we pay enough for it as it is."

I glared up at the motivational posters on the walls. Ivy was twiddling her thumbs in the chair beside me. "It'll be completely educational. Mrs Knight said we're going to learn about nature."

I could almost see Edith smirk. "Oh yes, I'm sure looking at trees will be invaluable for your future. Will it help you to get a husband or pay your way in the world?"

I must have pulled a hideous face in response, because Ivy started silently laughing. What could I say to that? My mind raced. "But what if—"

"I said NO, Scarlet. You're staying at Rookwood. Where you belong."

There was a click as the line cut off.

"Well, at least I'm far away from YOU, you hideous old bat!" I screeched into the receiver, slamming it down.

Ivy looked horrified. "Scarlet, you didn't..."

I turned to her. "She hung up," I explained.

"Oh, thank goodness," she said.

I frowned at the telephone, as if it were responsible for all our problems. This was quite the setback.

"Are you sure you want to go on this trip?" Ivy asked, suddenly.

Was she mad? "Of course! We've wanted to get away from Rookwood this whole time, haven't we?"

I half expected my twin to bring up the fact that it was at least preferable to being locked in an asylum, as I had been when Miss Fox had convinced everyone I was crazy. But she didn't say that, and there was a faraway look in her eyes. "I've just got a bad feeling about this," she said hazily. Then she blinked and came back to reality. "Maybe it's more trouble than it's worth. Edith is never going to agree to it."

"I bet she would if we bribed her," I growled. We were almost certain that our stepmother had accepted a bribe from Miss Fox to keep quiet about the asylum incident.

"Perhaps we should just give up," Ivy replied, and she looked strangely hopeful.

"Give up? Since when do we *just give up*?" I said. "No. We'll think of something."

Friday's assembly brought letters. I shuffled in my seat as Mrs Knight called out the names, and each person went up to collect their post as others filed out of the hall.

Ariadne's name was called, and she came rushing back looking like an excited puppy. "Daddy's given me permission!" she said, flapping the letter at us. "I can go on the trip!" I think she noticed our downcast faces, because she slowly stopped flapping the paper. "Ah," she said. "You didn't get a letter, did you?"

Ivy shook her head. "Our stepmother is determined to stop us from going."

"Well, rats," said Ariadne. "I'm not sure if I want to go on my own."

I looked around at the other girls in our year. Nadia appeared to be celebrating, so I supposed her parents had agreed to let her go. Penny was slumped in her seat looking dejected. I almost felt sorry for her, but... no, I wasn't quite there yet. Not after all her bullying.

"You might avoid being stuck with Penny, at least. It looks like her parents haven't given their permission," I said.

We stood up to head for the first lesson, but someone was in the way, blocking our exit from the row.

"You're going on the trip, then, are you, Flitworth?" It was Elsie Sparks, the prissy prefect, flanked by two others whose names I didn't know. Their shiny prefect badges glinted on their lapels.

"Yes, I am," Ariadne said, clutching her letter to her dress.

"Hmm," Elsie smirked at her friends. "Another one we've got to keep an eye on. They're trouble this lot." Her eyes flicked over to me and Ivy. "But I didn't see a letter for you two, did I? Are you leaving her to come all alone?"

"Actually—" Ivy started, but I interrupted her.

"Actually we *will* be going. Just as soon as we get the permission slip. It probably got lost in the post."

"Ha!" snorted Elsie. "I'm sure it did."

One of the other prefects beside her peered at me down her nose. She was very tall, with unreasonably long legs and perfectly curled short brown hair. Her satchel was neatly labelled CASSANDRA CLARKSON, so I presumed that was her name, unless she'd pinched the bag from someone else. "I know you two," she said, in a voice that sounded like it was giving us an exam. "You're the twins who got rid of the headmaster, aren't you?"

"Yes," I said. "What's your point?"

"Hmmph," she sniffed. "I liked him. He chose me as a prefect, after all."

Mr Bartholomew, the old head, had tried to bring back the prefect system when he took over the school back from Miss Fox. His choices were utterly terrible, but the teachers wouldn't be picking new prefects until next year.

Ivy gaped at Cassandra, while I just stared daggers at her. She was mad if she actually liked the old man. "He *murdered* a student!" Ivy pointed out.

"Well, perhaps she should have behaved," the tall girl said with a wry smile.

Elsie smacked her on the arm. "You're such a card, Cassie!"

Cassandra giggled, as if she'd been terribly funny. I

wanted to give her a smack myself, but it would have been a lot harder, and probably round the face area.

"Right," I said. "Will you lot get out of our way so we can get to class?" I wasn't particularly in a rush to learn, but I was fed up with being taunted.

The other prefect, who had dark hair and a horse-riding rosette pinned to her uniform, spread her arms out wide. "Is that any way to talk to your betters?"

"Oh, for goodness' sake," I said. I wasn't about to let them walk all over us. I pushed the horsey girl out of the way and stomped into the aisle. Ivy and Ariadne darted behind me.

"Watch it, Grey," Elsie hissed, as her friend dusted herself off in mock horror. "We'll be keeping an eye on your little friend on the trip, and you wouldn't want her to get into trouble, would you?" She glanced pointedly at Ariadne, who gulped.

At that moment, Mrs Knight headed across the quickly emptying hall towards us. "Problem, girls?" she asked.

"Oh, none at all, Miss," said Elsie, pulling out her cheerful sucking-up-to-teachers voice. "We were simply telling these little ones how *excited* we are about the trip. It's going to be *so* wonderful!"

Mrs Knight beamed. I clenched my fists to prevent myself from punching anyone.

"How lovely to see some school spirit again," the headmistress said happily. "Right then, off to lessons with you all."

I wasn't about to be told twice, so I grabbed Ivy and Ariadne's hands and we hurried away from the prefects.

"I can't believe Mrs Knight is putting those smarmy slugs in charge," I muttered as we walked through the corridors.

"Me neither," said Ivy. It had been bad enough going for a short bus ride with Elsie last term, let alone having to suffer a whole week of her bossing us about.

Ariadne had gone a bit pale. "Please don't leave me alone with them," she said.

"We won't," I promised. "We'll find a way."

But at that moment, I had to admit – I was out of ideas.

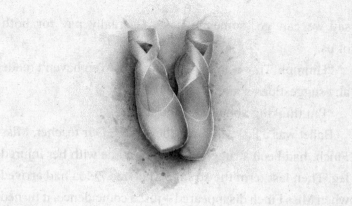

Chapter Three

Ivy

I was afraid of going on the trip, I had to admit. I felt sure something was going to go wrong, just as it always did. But what I was even more worried about was leaving Ariadne in the company of unscrupulous prefects for a week. Scarlet was right. We had to get permission. But how?

"We could forge a letter from our parents!" Scarlet suggested as we walked to ballet that afternoon.

"That's just a recipe for trouble if we get found out," I said. "Not to mention that they don't just have to say we can go, someone has to actually pay for both of us."

"Hmmph," my twin folded her arms. "You haven't made any suggestions so far."

"I'm thinking about it," I insisted.

Ballet was a little different these days. Our teacher, Miss Finch, had been struggling for some time with her injured leg. Then last term the strange Madame Zelda had arrived when Miss Finch disappeared – just a coincidence, it turned out, as Zelda had actually turned up hoping to apologise for being the one to cause the injury.

They must have had a long talk, because now they seemed happy to be in the same room as one another – or at the very least, they accepted it. Mrs Knight had decided that it would be best for them to share the job of teaching ballet in order to give Miss Finch a bit of a rest now and then.

We descended the steps into the chilly basement ballet studio, where Miss Finch and Madame Zelda were waiting. Miss Finch sat at the piano, while Zelda stood staring into the mirror. They weren't talking, but the atmosphere didn't seem too unfriendly.

"Ah, girls," said Madame Zelda as we walked in. "Begin your warm-up, please."

We started lacing on our shoes, never quite sure whether

we had to remain silent as Madame Zelda usually insisted, or whether we could talk more freely as Miss Finch had let us in the past. I watched as Nadia and another girl came down the stairs into the room.

"I'm just so excited for the trip," Nadia was saying. "A whole week away from school!"

Madame Zelda looked at her sharply. "I hope you will be practising extra hard this week, then, Miss Sayani. You don't want to get behind with your ballet."

Nadia straightened up. "No, Miss!" she said.

The new teacher seemed pleased with her answer. "Good. And you two? Will you be leaving us as well?" she asked, looking down at me and Scarlet.

"Couldn't get permission," said Scarlet, glaring at the floor. "Awful parents."

"I can sympathise," called Miss Finch from the piano.

I got to my feet, and Madame Zelda placed a thin hand lightly on my shoulder. "Then we shall enjoy having you both in class," she said, and winked at me.

I tried to smile, but Scarlet looked so miserable that I couldn't quite manage it.

Penny walked in then, and Madame Zelda turned to her. "What about you, Miss Winchester? Will you be going on this trip?"

Penny's expression turned thunderous. "No," she said.

"And why's that?" asked Madame Zelda, her face inquisitive and open.

To my surprise, Penny actually answered her honestly. "My parents haven't replied to the letter. And I don't think they're going to. I thought of writing to my uncle to see if he might pay for me to go, but..." She trailed off, and looked around at us. "It's none of your business, anyway," she finished.

"Careful," Madame Zelda said, waving her finger. "We must have the composure of a ballet dancer, mustn't we?"

Penny sighed and slumped down to lace her shoes on. "Yes, Miss. Sorry, Miss."

Scarlet rolled her eyes, but something Penny had said stuck in my mind as we began doing our stretches. *I thought of writing to my uncle*. The thought grew bigger and bigger. We had two aunts now, aunts who were both kind and generous. If we wrote to them...

At the end of the lesson, I grabbed Scarlet. "I think we should write to Aunt Phoebe and Aunt Sara about the trip!"

"Why?" My twin wrinkled her nose. "To tell them our stepmother is the spawn of the devil? I think they already know that."

"No," I said. "To ask them for permission. They might be able to pay the fees for us."

Scarlet's eyes widened. "Is that allowed?"

"I have no idea." I thought about it for a moment. "I'm hoping Aunt Phoebe might have been listed as a guardian on our records."

Scarlet started to grin. "You're a genius. Let's try it!"

We composed the letters that night. We wrote to both Aunt Sara and Aunt Phoebe, telling them all about the trip and asking if we could go.

"We'll go to the village first thing tomorrow and post them," said Scarlet. "They won't take long to get there."

I crossed my fingers. Ariadne was sitting on my bed and nervously knitting. "I hope they say yes," she said, twirling the wool round her fingers.

"Me too," I said. "If we don't get permission by Friday, then we'll be taken off the list."

We had to do it. I didn't want our stepmother to win again.

Friday dawned, and I was desperate for assembly to start – because Friday's assembly meant letters.

I ran into Rose in the corridor as I headed for the lavatories, feeling chilly in my nightgown. She was leaving the room she had shared with Violet, her face forlorn as she slowly pulled the door closed. Violet and Rose had been inseparable after meeting in the asylum. She must miss her.

Rose was unusual to say the least – she was an enigma, and rumours abounded throughout the school. We knew very little about her. She wasn't one to talk, usually, and when she did, she spoke so softly that you had to strain to hear her.

"Good morning, Rose," I said brightly.

She smiled at me.

"Did you hear about the trip?" I asked, carrying on walking as she came up beside me.

She nodded.

"Our stepmother wouldn't give us permission," I explained, "but we're going to ask our aunts. I hope we'll be able to go. Well, I was worried about going at first, but I think Ariadne needs us."

As we reached the lavatories, I started to worry that we were having a bit of a one-sided conversation. At least, more one-sided than usual. "Do you think you'd like to go?"

Rose looked back in the direction of her room. "I would," she whispered. "Very much. Only…"

She trailed off, but I could fill in the gaps. She didn't have Violet any more, and she wasn't a proper student. Even more than that, there was no one who could give her permission.

"I'm sorry," I said. "I didn't think. It's not long, though. Only a week." We went inside, and I washed my face with the freezing-cold water from the sink.

She smiled again, but she seemed sad. If only there was something we could do. But if we couldn't get on the trip ourselves, I didn't see how we'd be able to take Rose.

After breakfast, we headed for assembly. Scarlet pretty much bounced into her seat, dropping her satchel on the floor and nudging it about with her foot. She was so jittery, waiting to see if we'd got a letter. I was too. I barely listened to what Mrs Knight was telling us.

"Now," Mrs Knight said, "don't forget that today is the deadline for your permission letters." My ears pricked up, and Scarlet squeezed my knee. "On that note," the headmistress said, "it's post day."

She began reading out names from the pile of letters in her hand. "Agatha Brown! Alice Carter-Jones!"

Scarlet squeezed my knee even harder as the alphabet got closer to our surname. I had to slap her hand away, because I didn't want my leg to fall off.

"Scarlet and Ivy Grey!"

Scarlet leapt up and ran for the stage. She grabbed the letter from Mrs Knight's hand and was back in her seat tearing open the envelope before I even had time to speak.

I read it over her shoulder. I didn't recognise the beautiful looped handwriting, but I soon realised it must belong to our Aunt Sara.

Dear Scarlet and Ivy,

My darlings, I hope you are well. I received your letter about the school trip. I have managed to speak to your Aunt Phoebe (it wasn't easy - I had to telephone someone named Philip?).

We have decided that you ought to be allowed to go on the trip. We'll keep this quiet from Edith, shall we? I have enclosed a cheque for you, which should be more than enough to cover the trip, and a letter of permission.

Go forth, my darlings, and have a new adventure!

With love,

Sara Louise

Chapter Four

SCARLET

I started bouncing up and down in the middle of the hall. I couldn't believe it. We were going on the trip! Finally, a way out of Rookwood – even if it was only for a week.

"Aunt Sara is the best!" I said. I was so glad we'd found her. At least someone was on our side who could help us. Aunt Phoebe was lovely too, but she couldn't be trusted to remember where she'd left her own head.

Ariadne was bouncing beside me. "It's going to be brilliant!" she cried.

Ivy wasn't quite bouncing, but she at least looked pleased. "We need to take this to Mrs Knight," she said.

"No time like the present," I said. I ran to the front of the hall, where Mrs Knight was just stepping down from the stage. "Miss! We can go on the trip!" I waved the letter and the cheque at her.

Mrs Knight held her hands out in front of her protectively. "Slow down a moment, Scarlet. Let me see."

I handed the papers over, and she pulled her glasses up from the chain round her neck and put them on. I watched as her eyes slid along each line of the letter.

"Well," she said after a moment. "This is a little irregular. I do recall your aunts, but..."

"Aunt Sara's paid the fees!" I said, tapping the cheque repeatedly.

An expression I couldn't quite read crossed Mrs Knight's face. She took her glasses back off again. "Ah. Hmm. I suppose it's all right..."

"Yes!" I punched the air.

Ivy came up beside me. "Thank you, Miss," she said.

"Um, yes," said Mrs Knight, taking the cheque from me and tucking it into her pocket. She patted it a few times, as if making sure it was still there. "Well done, girls. The bus leaves at four o'clock on Monday." She wandered away, leaving us both to share an excited hug.

Ariadne had ceased bouncing by this point, and now she looked a little concerned. "I just remembered about Rose," she said. "Do you think she stands any chance?"

I shrugged. "No idea. She doesn't have parents who can give her permission..."

"...but she doesn't have parents to deny her permission either," Ivy finished. That was a good point. I wasn't sure what Mrs Knight would say to that.

"But the trip is full anyway," I said, picking up my satchel from the floor. "Miss Bowler made it very clear that your name has to be down. I don't think there's anything we can do."

Ariadne sighed. "You're probably right. Poor Rose."

I felt sorry for her as well. Violet had been Rose's best friend, and at the moment it didn't look like Violet was coming back. And all right, I was a little *pleased* about that. She'd always wanted everything to go her way, and I wanted everything to go *my* way, and that was always going to be a recipe for disaster.

Still, Rose didn't deserve to lose her friend. She was so shy and quiet and kind, completely the opposite of Vile Violet. She'd been through the same asylum hell that I'd been through. But most people still thought she was strange and avoided her, or at worst, picked on her. I didn't want to abandon her at school with only the horses to talk to.

"We can get someone nice to keep an eye on her," I

suggested. "But right now we have more important things to do."

"Oh?" Ivy said with a curious smile.

"Like PACKING!"

"We have lessons," Ariadne pointed out.

"I know," I said. "But after that, we can start packing. Because WE'RE GOING ON THE TRIP!"

I raced through Rookwood's traditional stew dinner that night. As soon as we were back in room thirteen, I pulled my old battered suitcase out from under the bed. I tossed it on to the blankets and opened it wide, taking a moment to appreciate the possibilities.

Ivy was looking at me funny.

"What?" I asked.

"What are we supposed to pack?" she said. She waved a list that we'd been given of things we were meant to bring. "We can't wear uniform, but we don't have most of these things. *Hiking clothes?*"

Ugh. She was right. We'd picked up a few things when we'd briefly returned home, but the sad truth was that most of my clothes had been taken away when they'd thought I was dead. And our parents had never provided us with much in the first place.

"We'll just have to take what we have. Can I borrow some

of yours?" I asked. That was one advantage of being a twin. We both wore the same size.

She sighed. "All right. Let's have a look." She went over to the wardrobe and pulled it open.

I followed and peered over her shoulder. It contained our ballet outfits, a few plain dresses and skirts that belonged to Ivy, and one that belonged to me. Oh, and the embarrassing costumes that Ariadne had made us, but I wasn't planning on ever wearing one of *those* again.

I moved Ivy out of the way and grabbed my dress and a couple of hers. "Scarlet!" she moaned.

"What?" I said. "I'm only borrowing them." I made a show of folding them as neatly as possible and placing them gently in the suitcase.

There was a knock at the door and Ariadne bounded in. She was clutching the camera again.

"I've been asked to take photographs!" she said, grinning with excitement.

"Oh no," I said, putting my hands up to protect myself. "No more posing!"

"No, silly, not of you. Of everyone. On the trip." She made a sweeping gesture at the window, as if that conveyed everything.

"Really?" Ivy asked. "I thought the teachers didn't like you using the camera?"

"Mrs Knight asked me personally," Ariadne said, her chest swelling with pride. "She wants to take lots of pictures for the school newsletter, and they might put some in the local paper as well."

The local paper? "Goodness," said Ivy, sitting down at the desk. "She really is determined to promote the school with this, isn't she?"

"Well, make sure you get my good side," I said.

"You have a good side?" Ivy asked, puzzled. And then added after a moment, "but we're mirror twins. Does that mean it's my bad side?"

To be honest, I didn't have a clue. It was just something that I'd heard people say. I changed the subject. "What are you going to bring, Ariadne?"

"Oh, all sorts," said Ariadne, and she winked at me. It was a bit strange seeing her attempt to wink. What was that all about? I'd have to ask her later.

I went over to our desk drawer, which now contained various school books and ink pens alongside Ivy's pearl necklace and my hairbrush – the only heirlooms we'd inherited from our mother. I'd always thought they were a strange choice, but they'd actually helped us crack the mystery of her true identity and discover Aunt Sara. I stroked the necklace gently. "You should bring this along," I said to Ivy, pulling it out. "Maybe we'll get to have a grand dinner in the hotel." It was usually against the rules to wear jewellery at Rookwood, but if we weren't *at* Rookwood then I didn't think the rules applied.

Ivy smiled and took it from me. "Maybe," she said. "I'll have to be careful with it, though." She pulled out her own carpet bag from the bottom of the wardrobe and gently lowered the necklace in.

I packed the hairbrush, along with the Rookwood regulation toothbrush and threadbare towel we were all given. I wasn't sure if we were allowed to take those away (or even if the hotel would have their own – we'd never been to a hotel before) but they were the only ones I had, so they were going in.

Ivy pulled out a pen and paper. "We must write to our aunts and thank them," she said. "I still can't believe they've sent us the money to go."

I nodded. "I can't believe we're going," I said. I slammed the suitcase shut and started jumping up and down on it. "This is going to be the best week ever!"

Chapter Five

Ivy

The day of the trip arrived, and Scarlet was awake even before the morning bell had rung. As my eyes creaked open, I watched her leap out of bed and pull her suitcase from beneath it.

"Scarlet," I managed, half asleep. "We're not leaving until this afternoon."

"So?" she said with a mischievous grin. "Our motto is 'be prepared', is it not?"

I pushed myself up and threw my pillow at her. "You're

thinking of the Scouts. The Rookwood motto is 'Nothing is heavy for those who have wings'."

She tossed the pillow back at me and tried to pick up her suitcase. "Ouch. Whoever came up with that obviously never tried to lift this."

I blinked sleepily. "I thought you had barely anything to pack? How did it get so heavy?"

She bent down, undid the metal catches and flipped the leather lid open. The suitcase had acquired several jars of sweets.

"Ariadne gave me some of her stash," Scarlet said. "For emergencies. She said she didn't have room for all of it."

I didn't think anyone had ever had to have an emergency midnight feast, but I wouldn't put it past Ariadne.

We got dressed and headed down for breakfast. We still had a morning of lessons to get through, but even that couldn't put the brakes on Scarlet's excitement. "Only eight hours to go!" she said as she collected her porridge in the dining hall. "Then it's goodbye porridge and goodbye Rookwood!"

I grinned at her. "We're coming back, though," I pointed out.

"I can pretend that we aren't," she retorted.

Scarlet's enthusiasm was catching. It really would be

great to get away from Rookwood for a little while, and to see somewhere new.

At midday, Scarlet grabbed my arm. "It's midday!" she whispered.

"What does that mean?" I shot back.

"It means there's only four hours to go!"

I laughed. I hoped this trip could live up to her expectations.

Finally, *finally*, it was time for us to head out to the front of the school and watch for the bus. In fact we were rather early, but I thought that if we waited any longer Scarlet would burst.

We sat on the steps with our luggage. The sun was bright and warm where it spilt on to the stone, and the air was filled with the cawing of the rooks. One of them darted to the ground and tipped its head to the side, inspecting us. Another hopped down next to it.

I'd read about them in a book on birds once. It said that one of the names for a group of rooks was a *parliament*. I told Scarlet this.

She pointed at one and said: "Is that a Member of Parliament, then?"

The rook didn't look pleased. It squawked at her and then took flight, its wings beating patterns in the warm air.

We stared at the rooks for a while longer before I heard the school's enormous doors being pulled open, and Ariadne appeared at the top of the steps. She was dragging two large suitcases that seemed to match the little convoy she'd brought on the very first day of school. She left them propping open the door and came down to us.

I looked up at her, putting my hand over my eyes to shield them from the sun. "That can't all be sweets in there?" I asked, baffled.

She blinked at me. "Oh! No! This is mostly my camera equipment. I'm hoping there might be somewhere dark I can develop the photographs while we're there."

I had no idea whether hotels usually had a darkroom, but it seemed unlikely.

She stepped down on to the drive, took the camera out of the case round her neck and pointed it at us. "Smile!"

I smiled as the lens clicked and whirred. I think Scarlet pulled a face.

"Oh, hello, Rose," Ariadne said. "I think you got in the picture."

I twisted round and saw Rose standing behind us.

"Where did you come from?" Scarlet asked. Rose just smiled knowingly.

Talking to Rose was often a bit of a guessing game. "Did you come to say goodbye to us?" Ariadne asked.

She nodded and smiled, but her smile seemed sad. I watched her twisting the chain of her golden locket round her fingers, as she often seemed to do as a nervous habit. "I wish I could go," she said quietly.

Suddenly, we heard shouting coming from the entrance hall.

Scarlet stood up. "What on earth is going on in there?"

We all ran back inside, leaving our luggage behind while Rose just stared off into the distance. Some drama was clearly unfolding.

As my eyes adjusted to the light indoors, I saw Mrs Knight standing in front of one of Elsie's prefect friends. The headmistress's arms were crossed in a very clear display of displeasure.

"Calm down, please, Betty," she was saying.

"This isn't fair!" The girl screeched at her. "I'm a prefect! I've got to go!"

Mrs Knight didn't budge. "You aren't *entitled* to go. Mr Bartholomew chose you as a prefect, yes, but you've forged your permission letter." She glanced over at the new Rookwood secretary on the front desk, a lady named Miss Jarvis, who had slanted spectacles and always looked a little annoyed. I wondered if she'd been the one to discover the forgery. "That is unacceptable behaviour, as is the fuss you are making right now."

I gulped nervously. Thank goodness we hadn't tried forgery.

Betty scrunched her hands into her dark hair as if she were about to pull it out. "I paid the fees out of my own pocket! You *have* to let me on that bus!"

The headmistress was frowning intently, which was about as angry as she got. If Miss Fox had been there, Betty would have been dragged off for a caning before her feet could touch the ground. "You can have your money back, but you have broken the rules, madam, and now you will have to live with the consequences. And you can have a detention for talking to me in that manner too."

Betty clenched her fists and stormed off without another word, leaving us all there staring after her. Mrs Knight sighed, though I couldn't tell if it was frustration or relief.

As Betty left the room, she nearly bumped into Miss Bowler, who was striding in carrying an enormous bag. "Watch where you're going, Smith!" Miss Bowler bellowed after her. She dropped the bag on the floor with a thud and then appeared to notice all of our startled faces. "Something the matter?"

"Miss Smith forged her permission slip," Mrs Knight said, her voice heavy with disappointment. "She is no longer coming with us."

"Well, I never!" said Miss Bowler. "Students these days! They think they can get away with anything..."

As Miss Bowler ranted to a somewhat stunned Mrs Knight, Scarlet pulled Ariadne and me into a circle. "I've just had an idea..." she said, keeping her voice lowered.

"What is it?" I asked.

"Betty's off the trip. But her space has already been booked," Scarlet began.

"But we're about to leave," Ariadne said, flapping her arms. "Nobody's going to get permission from their parents now!"

"Yes," said Scarlet. She looked pointedly out of the vast open doors of the school. "But what about someone who doesn't have parents to ask?"

I suddenly saw what she meant. This was Rose's chance to join the trip!

"Oh, Scarlet," Ariadne grinned. "That's brilliant. Go and ask!"

"You're coming with me." Scarlet grabbed us by one arm each, and tugged us over to where the two teachers stood.

"...and that's why they should bring back the stocks!" Miss Bowler finished, with a final flourish of her muscular arms. Then she noticed us. "Yes?"

"Is there a problem, girls?" Mrs Knight asked.

"Mi-iss," said Scarlet, in the voice she used when she

was trying to get something from a teacher. "We couldn't help but overhear that a place has just become available... and we wanted to ask if Rose could come?"

"*Who's Rose?*" said Miss Bowler in a pantomime whisper to Mrs Knight.

"The girl who helps at the stables," the headmistress said, as this was the way most people referred to Rose these days.

"Oh, right, right," Miss Bowler said. "The funny one who's forgotten how to talk."

Mrs Knight frowned. "Well, I'm not sure about this..."

"You said the hotel's already been booked," Ariadne pointed out. "And you don't need to ask her parents because she doesn't have any."

Mrs Knight looked questioningly at Miss Bowler, but the swimming instructor just shrugged at her. "All right, I suppose she might as well. Your aunt sent a very generous sum that would more than pay for Rose's place, in fact. Well, tell her to go and get her things, then. Quickly now."

Scarlet took this a bit too literally, and turned round to face the outside with her hands cupped to her mouth. "ROSE!" she yelled. "MRS KNIGHT SAYS YOU CAN HAVE BETTY'S PLACE ON THE TRIP! GO AND GET YOUR THINGS!"

Which was entirely the wrong moment, because as Rose

spun round in surprise, Elsie Sparks walked in. And she looked *furious*.

Elsie went right up to Mrs Knight, not even looking at us. "Miss," she said quietly. "Is it true? Betty is off the trip? She just came to me sobbing."

The headmistress was clearly losing her patience. "*Yes*, Elsie. Betty broke the rules. We're taking Miss... Rose instead. Now if you'll excuse me, we need to go and meet the bus." She hurried off out of the front doors, Miss Bowler striding after her.

Now Elsie was glaring in our direction. "You little rats," she said.

"What?" I replied. "What did we do?"

"Betty should be coming with us. Not your weird silent friend. You'd all better watch your backs!" And with that, she swung her bag up on to her shoulder and stalked off outside.

Ariadne stared after her. "Should we be worried?"

"She should be afraid of us," said Scarlet, clenching her fists. "I'm going to get Rose and we're going to have a great time. Elsie Sparks can go hang."

The bus had arrived, the same one that had taken us to the ballet last term. It smelt of leather seats and petrol.

Scarlet had taken Rose to get her few possessions, which largely consisted of things that Violet had stolen for her which hadn't been claimed back. I think the only things she truly owned were the clothes she stood up in and the golden locket that hung round her neck.

Ariadne and I had climbed on board, lifting our bags into the luggage racks above our heads (Ariadne's took us several attempts, since it seemed to be full of bricks). We sat near the back, as far away from Elsie and her friend Cassandra as possible, since they were already shooting glares at us. Mrs Knight was standing at the front of the bus, holding the list of names up like a shield as she tried to sort out who was supposed to be there and who wasn't. Already some girls had tried unsuccessfully to get on board and Miss Bowler had sent them packing with detentions.

Nearly all the seats filled up, except the two beside us that we had saved.

Ariadne looked at her watch. "It's time to go!" she said. "Where are Scarlet and Rose?"

Typical, I thought. Scarlet had been the one counting down the seconds until this trip and now she was late. "Come on," I whispered out of the window.

Miss Bowler climbed on board. "Who are we missing?" she bellowed down the aisle. "Grey and... whatsername?"

"Yes, Miss," I piped up. "They'll be here soon!"

"They'd better be," she muttered, but even a mutter from Miss Bowler was rather loud. "The driver is waiting."

I peered down the aisle at the driver, who was a fairly young man in a flat cap. He didn't look like he was waiting. He looked like he was quite enjoying reading his newspaper and eating a biscuit.

After a few anxious minutes of staring at the front steps, I spotted Scarlet dragging Rose behind her. "Thank goodness," I said. I was pleased to see that Rose was smiling.

"Hurry up, girls!" I could hear Mrs Knight saying as she waved them on. They hopped up the steps and headed towards us. Elsie whispered something to Cassandra as they passed. I couldn't hear, but I was sure it wasn't very nice.

Scarlet and Rose took the two seats we'd saved for them on the other side of the aisle, and Scarlet lifted their bags up. Rose waved at us happily.

Finally Mrs Knight stepped on. "Are we all here?"

"Yes!" everyone chorused, somewhat pointlessly.

"Right, then! Off to Lake Seren we go!" She pumped her fist in the air and then climbed into the front seat beside Miss Bowler.

The driver looked back at her. "Can I finish my biscuit first?" he said.

Chapter Six

SCARLET

The bus pulled out of Rookwood's gates. As the stone rooks swept past us, I squeezed Ivy's hand across the aisle. I knew this trip was going to be brilliant.

We chugged along the country roads, past the miles of hedgerows and open fields and oak trees. The afternoon sun made the bus swelteringly hot, and I started to wish I had a drink.

At one point Nadia tried to begin a singalong, but Elsie

swiftly told her to shut up. At least there was one thing we agreed upon.

I started telling Rose what I thought we'd get up to on the trip. "It's a really grand hotel," I said. "Incredibly posh. I imagine we'll be drinking champagne and bathing in milk. Or is that the other way round?"

Rose giggled.

"And there will probably be dancing and lawn tennis and croquet," I carried on. I was pretty sure that was the sort of thing they did at hotels.

"Will there be horses?" Rose asked quietly.

"Definitely," I said, though I had no idea. "Probably with glass carriages and footmen."

The bus carried on, and soon everyone had pulled open the tiny windows above the seats.

"It's so hot," Ivy moaned.

"I'm boiling," Ariadne said, blowing away a lock of hair that kept trying to stick to her face.

I pointed out of the window. The sun was lower in the sky now, slipping behind the trees. "The sun will set soon. Then we'll hopefully stop melting." I was sticking to my seat.

Ariadne nodded and yawned. Moments later, she'd fallen asleep.

The landscape started to change around us. We passed

through a town I didn't recognise, all red brick and smoking chimneys. Then there was more countryside, dappled with houses here and there. The sunset washed the sky with orange and a deep blood red.

"Are we there yet?!" someone yelled, making everyone laugh. Ariadne awoke with a jolt and nearly hit Ivy in the face with a flailing arm.

"Miles to go before we sleep," said Mrs Knight.

I sighed. Everyone had been quiet until that point, mostly just staring out at the darkening road. My excitement wasn't draining; it was more like just... postponed. Being kept on hold for when we got there.

Twilight fell, and brought cooler air with it. I wondered where we were. The sloping hills of the countryside I knew were starting to look more like mountains. There were stone walls and pine trees and bubbling streams.

Some time later, the bus drove between two enormous rocks, and I spotted a waterfall cascading down the side of a cliff. I could hear the rushing water over the roar of the engine. "Rose, over there!" I nudged her, and she looked where I was pointing and smiled. We were quite high up, I realised, and as we rounded a corner I saw why. We were on the edge of the valley, overlooking the vast lake. "There it is!"

I glanced over at Ariadne and Ivy to see if they were awake. Ariadne looked like she had nodded off, but Ivy was staring out of the back window of the bus. I poked her arm. "What are you looking at?"

"There are headlamps behind us," she said, a concerned expression on her face. "That car's been there a long time, I swear it."

"Never mind that," I said. "Look at the lake!"

I spoke loudly enough that I not only woke Ariadne again, but several other people nearby snapped to attention and peered out at the lake.

It was getting dark, but the landscape was still visible. The lake was huge, and looked a deep navy blue against the black of the hills. "Is that a tower?" I said, pointing at a shadowy structure rising out of the water. Rose nodded. She looked fascinated.

"There's lights," said Ariadne, squinting out at the darkness. I wasn't sure if she was entirely awake.

"What?" I said.

"Lights under the lake," she replied. "Near the tower."

I couldn't see what she was talking about, and then, just for a moment, I thought I saw a flash of *something*.

"Hmm," Ivy said.

We all watched the surface of the water as the bus descended the hill, but I couldn't spot anything else. The road became bumpier as we went along and I was nearly jolted out of my seat.

As I righted myself, I heard Rose gasp. The bus was pulling out on to an enormous stone bridge. Everyone stood up to get a better look.

"Sit down, girls," I heard Mrs Knight warn sleepily, but I didn't listen to her. I saw the dark water spreading out in all directions around us.

"There's the hotel!" Nadia cried, pointing.

I could see it, a big shadow on the landscape with flickering lights in the windows. "We're almost there!"

The bus crossed the bridge, and the first few stars began to wink in the sky as I stared out. After what felt like an age, we reached the other side of the lake and the bus started climbing again, up to where the hotel stood.

"Right, everyone," Mrs Knight called, sounding a little more alert. "We're very close to the Shady Pines Hotel now." I could see where it got its name. The pine trees surrounded us on all sides. "I'm sure they'll give us a lovely, warm welcome!"

And then the bus slowly came to a halt. The car that had been following behind roared past us, making everyone jump.

We'd stopped next to a sign that I could just make out. It was peeling and cracked, and hung on a wooden pole with hinges that were creaking in the wind.

SHADY PINES HOTEL
Furnished rooms to rent
Please enjoy your stay

At least, I thought that was what it was meant to say. Three of the letters had worn away from the bottom line, making it look more like it said *Pleas enjo your sty*.

"Can't you go right up to the door?" I heard Mrs Knight say to the driver.

He stood up. "The engine's gone," he said. "Too steep. Going to have to roll it back down the hill to start it. Can I drop you all off here?"

Mrs Knight sighed. "All right, girls! Everyone off! Don't forget to pick up your bags!"

"But, Miss," I heard someone moan sleepily from the front.

"No buts!" said Miss Bowler. "Off!"

We all began sluggishly pulling our things down from the luggage rack. "I can't believe they're making us walk up there," I said to Rose as I stared out into the dark. She shivered and wrapped her cardigan tighter round herself. At least it was a clear night and we had the moon to see by.

We made our way to the front of the bus, Ivy and Ariadne not far behind, and stepped down. There was a chill in the air and the road was bumpy beneath my feet. I was about to complain some more, but I saw the horrified expressions on Elsie and Cassandra's faces and decided the discomfort was worth it.

Miss Bowler took charge. "Everyone here? Right! Off we go! No dilly-dallying!"

"The hotel looks a bit... old," muttered Ariadne as we began to trudge up the hill with our bags.

"Perhaps it looks better in the daylight," Ivy replied optimistically. I grabbed her hand. I didn't mind the dark, but even now I didn't like being alone in it. It reminded me too much of the past. And you never knew who might be lurking round the corner.

The hotel building was above us now, and I looked up at it. It was huge and gloomy, and I could just make out dark stone and pointed roofs, and what looked like oil lamps flickering in some of the windows.

Eventually the steep road curved round to the left and became a gravel driveway that crunched under our feet. The pine trees were everywhere, tall black shadows in the darkness.

"I'm cold," Nadia moaned.

Elsie whacked her on the arm when the teachers weren't looking. "Stop whining," she said.

I glared at her. What a hypocrite. She was a champion whiner!

The driveway eventually opened out into a sort of courtyard, with the hotel itself to the left of us, a lamp glowing in its front porch. There were a few motor cars parked outside. To the right was what looked like a stable yard and coach house, and I could hear a horse whinnying somewhere. Rose smiled.

We stopped in front of the porch. "Here we are!" said Mrs Knight, spreading her arms wide.

For goodness' sake, please don't give us another motivational speech, I thought. I was starving hungry, not to mention cold and tired. I just wanted to get inside. The hotel would have food and warmth and beds.

Thankfully, if Mrs Knight had been about to give a speech, it didn't happen, because Miss Bowler shouldered past her and made for the front door. It groaned open as if it hadn't been used in years, although I knew that couldn't be true.

The hotel reception was a wide room with a desk in the middle. There was a bell and an old-fashioned oil lamp on the desk, and not much else. Electricity hadn't reached the place yet, then.

As we huddled together on the plush carpet, Miss Bowler went right up to the desk and slammed her hand down on the bell about three times. For a full minute there was no answer, but eventually a man appeared from the door at the back.

He was fairly old, with greying hair and a stooped back, but he moved quickly. He wore a pair of golden spectacles. A smoking jacket and stiff shoes clung to him awkwardly. "Mm?" was all he said.

"We've arrived from Rookwood School," said Mrs Knight, going up to him with her clipboard. "We were hoping to check in."

The man looked at her as if she'd just asked him to polish her shoes. "It's rather late, madam," he said.

"Well, when I booked, I explained that—" Mrs Knight started, but Miss Bowler was having none of it.

"Never mind that!" she boomed. "We're here now!"

"This is most irregular," the man muttered as he pulled a hefty book out of the desk drawer. "Twice in one night! Guests thinking they can just *turn up* and..." His muttering got quieter until I could no longer hear what he was saying, which was probably a good thing. What a grumpy old man!

Ivy leant over. "I wonder who else turned up late?" she whispered, and I shrugged in reply.

The man turned the book round to face Mrs Knight. "Sign here, then. My wife will show you to your rooms shortly."

"Any chance of some grub?" asked Miss Bowler.

He lifted his gaze slowly and fixed her with a nasty glare that would rival my own. "The kitchen is long since closed, *madam.* You will have to go to the dining hall in the morning." With that, he slammed the guest book shut, turned on his heel and headed back through the door behind him.

"If that was a warm welcome," I said to Ivy, "I'd hate to see a cold one."

Chapter Seven

Ivy

We'd been waiting at least ten minutes before the door at the back of the room opened and the sound of raised voices blared out. A woman, who I thought must be the man's wife, came out of the door and shut it behind her (with quite some relief, I thought).

"Good evening," she said. She had a much friendlier face than her husband, though it currently looked red and flustered. She wore a plain dress with an apron, but expensive-looking earrings glinted beneath her greying hair. "I'm Mrs Rudge. I'll be showing you to your rooms. We usually have a girl to do this, but she's off sick." Her tone was apologetic, though I noticed she didn't actually say sorry for her husband's behaviour.

She looked around the room at all of us. Most people were sitting on their suitcases. Scarlet and I were leaning against a wall, while Rose and Ariadne were trying their best to share one striped armchair in the corner. The prefects were standing by the teachers with their arms folded, apparently trying to make it seem as though they were in charge too. From the look on Mrs Rudge's face, I suspected we weren't her usual type of clientele.

"Your rooms are on the top floor of the building," she said, pulling a bunch of jangling keys from a hook beside the door. I felt Scarlet twitch beside me.

"I don't suppose there's any chance of something to eat?" Mrs Knight asked, deciding to try a politer approach than Miss Bowler's.

Mrs Rudge nodded, though she didn't meet our teacher's eyes. "I can bring you up some bread and butter. I'm afraid that's all I can manage with the kitchen closed. My husband is very *particular* about these things."

Mrs Knight looked sympathetic. Miss Bowler looked like she was about to eat the reception desk.

"I'd love some bread and butter, actually," Scarlet said to me under her breath. "Much better than stew."

My stomach growled, and I had to agree.

"This way, please," said Mrs Rudge.

She led us out of the reception area and along a dark corridor which we all trod in a line, like ducks following their mother. We were too tired for chatter. The walls were dark wood, the carpets plush and red. There was a staircase, with sconces going up it – some of the candles lit, others not. I wondered if they'd never been lit in the first place, or if a draught had blown them out.

There were three floors, not unlike Rookwood, though I wasn't sure if the hotel was quite the size of our imposing school. But then it was dark, and how much of it had we actually seen? Once we'd made it to the top, Mrs Rudge went along unlocking all the doors and lighting the lamps, while Mrs Knight peered at her clipboard with the room assignments on it.

We leant against the wall as we waited for our names to be called. There were portraits running all the way down the stairs – portraits of long-dead strangers, as far as I could tell. I tried not to imagine that they were staring at me.

"Ivy Grey, Scarlet Grey," Mrs Knight called from further down the corridor. "Ariadne Flitworth and, erm..." she lowered the clipboard. "Rose?"

Rose's gaze flicked down to the floor, but she said nothing. If she had a surname, she wasn't giving it away.

"This one here, please," said Mrs Knight.

"That's not fair, Miss," Elsie whined as we made our way up the staircase past the other girls. "How come they get the big room? I thought it was ours?"

I was surprised that she'd made such an outburst in front of the teachers, but I supposed she was as tired as the rest of us. Luckily Miss Bowler was dropping off her bags into the teachers' room at the other end of the corridor at that point, otherwise she probably would've bellowed a reply and woken the whole hotel.

"I've tried to put everyone together with their friends," said Mrs Knight patiently. "And I've had to rearrange since we've lost Betty and gained Rose. No arguments, please."

"Yeah," said Scarlet, pulling a face at Elsie. "No arguments."

We took our bags over to the open door where Mrs Knight stood, and peered in.

The room was *huge*, much bigger than our dorm rooms back at school. Dark red striped wallpaper coated the walls, and heavy curtains hung at the windows. And the beds! There were two enormous four-poster beds, each with cream drapes.

"Oh my word," Scarlet exclaimed. It was the fanciest bedroom I'd ever seen, and I knew she was thinking the same.

"Oh, it looks just like my bedroom at home!" said Ariadne, beaming.

"Of course it does," said Scarlet, giving her a friendly jab in the arm.

Rose wandered in, staring around at everything, fascinated. I followed her and dropped my bag to the floor. It only took a moment for Scarlet to run in and start bouncing on the bed.

"Wheee!" she cried, the mattress creaking as she jumped.

Miss Bowler's face suddenly appeared in the doorway. "Stop that!"

Scarlet slowed her bouncing to a halt and then plopped down on to the covers. Miss Bowler marched on down the corridor.

There was furniture in the room too, big, heavy wooden pieces that looked like they were from the last century. And perhaps the strangest thing was a *bath*, in front of the windows. Not just a tin bath either, but a real bath with taps and silver clawed feet. "Look at this!" I said, walking over to it.

"Goodness," said Ariadne. "A bath in a bedroom? Well, I don't have that."

It looked quite old, and it reminded me a little of the baths at Rookwood, but it was more ornate and expensive-looking. I turned the tap to test it, and listened as the pipes clunked below. There was an empty moment, and then the water began to gush out. It was a slightly odd colour, with leafy fragments in it.

"Urgh," I said. "That doesn't look right."

Ariadne pointed out of the window. "Lake water, I think," she said. "It would make sense. I expect that's the easiest way to get it." I followed her finger and looked out at the view. Even in the dark it looked impressive – a vast body of black water, the moon shimmering on the surface.

"Yuck," said Scarlet. I looked over at her. She was now lying flat out on the bed like a starfish. "Do you think we have to drink that?"

"I expect they boil it first," said Ariadne hopefully. Rose giggled.

There was a knock at the open door, and we looked round to see Mrs Rudge standing there with a tray. "Some bread and butter for you, girls," she said. We all dashed over to her. I didn't think I'd ever seen Ariadne move so fast. "There will be more food tomorrow at breakfast."

We all took some and ate hungrily. It tasted marvellous – bread and butter was a rare treat, and it reminded me of living with Aunt Phoebe. I tried my best not to spill crumbs all over the plush carpet.

"I could get used to this," said Scarlet through a mouthful of bread.

"So which beds shall we take?" Ariadne asked when we'd finished munching.

"I think Scarlet's already claimed that one," I said, pointing at the one that had been thoroughly bounced on. "So I suppose that's me as well."

"Don't talk in your sleep," said Scarlet.

"Don't kick me!" I shot back.

"All right then," said Ariadne with a smile, "Rose and I will have this one."

"It's lovely." It took me a moment to realise who was speaking, since she was usually so silent. Rose was beaming. I supposed it wasn't long ago that all she'd had was an old straw mattress on the floor of the school basement, where Violet had hidden her. And before that, a hospital bed. And the rooms at Rookwood didn't exactly offer grand luxury either.

"LIGHTS OUT IN TEN MINUTES!" came a voice that was instantly recognisable as Miss Bowler's. "LAVATORIES ARE DOWN THE HALL!"

"Could you... keep it down a little, perhaps? We have other guests," I heard Mrs Rudge respond. I wasn't actually sure if Miss Bowler could, though. Loud seemed to be her natural volume. And were there other guests, even? I hadn't seen any.

We all pulled out our nightdresses and headed to the lavatories to get changed and brush our teeth. It turned out there weren't very many stalls, so there was quite a queue. By the time we got back to the room, someone had already put the lamp out.

"Thank goodness I brought supplies," said Ariadne. She dragged one of her small suitcases out towards the light of the corridor and pulled it open. It was full of candles.

Scarlet patted her on the back. "You're very strange, Ariadne, but it certainly comes in handy."

We huddled round the candle just inside the door of the room, and I suddenly noticed a glimmer of gold at Rose's neck.

My twin noticed it too. "You wear your locket to bed?"

Rose nodded and quickly tucked it away inside her borrowed nightgown, out of sight. Whatever was in that locket, it meant something to her.

Suddenly, Elsie Sparks appeared behind Ariadne. "Miss said lights out, you little weasels!" she snapped.

She blew out the candle and then slammed the door shut, plunging us into darkness.

Chapter Eight

SCARLET

I couldn't sleep.

I lay awake in the dark. The four-poster bed was warm and comfortable, much better than what I was used to, even if it was a little musty. But there was a chill coming from the fireplace, and I couldn't escape it without putting my head under the covers. And trying *that* had caused Ivy to prod me and whisper that I should stop messing around.

And on top of that, there had been the noises. Footsteps and dull banging and creaks from the walls. It was actually almost familiar – Rookwood was the same – but in a new place it was still unsettling.

Now Ivy was breathing steadily and twitching in her dreams, and I was pretty sure Ariadne was snoring. At least, someone was snoring, and Rose didn't seem like the type.

I sighed and rolled over. We hadn't shut the curtains, and there was a little moonlight, enough to cast the weird bath in shadow.

There was something odd about the Shady Pines Hotel, and whatever it was making me feel on edge. *Stop being so stupid*, I told myself. *You wanted to get away from Rookwood. And you're as far away from Miss Fox and the asylum as you'll ever be. Nothing is going to go wrong.*

That was when I heard a loud gasp from the corridor.

Well, *now* I was awake. I slipped out of the bed and over to the doorway, and pulled it open as gently as I could manage.

There were still lamps lit along the corridor, and Mrs Rudge was standing by the nearest one, staring at the wall opposite our door. She looked like she'd seen a ghost. Her face was pale and her hand was clamped over her mouth.

I shut the door gently behind me. "Mrs Rudge?"

She jumped and then turned to face me, lowering her hand. "Ah, Miss..." She trailed off, apparently realising she didn't actually know my name.

"Scarlet Grey," I said automatically. What had she seen? "Did something startle you?"

Her eyes flickered. "Well, you did, a little."

"I meant before that," I said. "I couldn't sleep and I heard you gasp."

"It was nothing," she said quickly. She straightened her apron. "I was coming to put out the lamps for the night, and I thought I saw a mouse; I'll, um... just finish putting these out, shall I?" She cupped her hand round the lamp and blew it out, and then hurried away to the next one.

I stepped into the corridor and examined the place she'd been staring at. There was a cross hanging from the wall. It was golden and quite ornate, and the nail it was dangling from looked haphazardly tapped in, like it was only just hanging on.

I frowned. I could've sworn that hadn't been there before. It seemed out of place among the portraits of posh dead people. Why on earth was Mrs Rudge so frightened of it? She didn't seem like a wet blanket – or at least I thought she couldn't be, not living in such a remote place with such a cranky husband. She had to be tougher than she looked. But a cross on the wall had just scared the stuffing out of her!

Maybe Mrs Rudge is a vampire and that's why she's afraid of crosses, I thought, chuckling to myself.

I had questions, but tiredness won. I was exhausted and the lights in the corridor were almost all out. I needed to go to bed before it became too dark to see.

I darted into the room and shut the door behind me, then felt my way to the bed. I jumped under the covers, relief washing over me.

Ivy rolled over. "You kicked me," she mumbled.

"And you're talking in your sleep," I said.

I woke the next morning feeling strangely light, like something was missing. My head swam with fog. As I pushed myself up on to the feather pillows, I realised what it was. There was no shrieking Rookwood morning bell!

Ivy had apparently noticed this as well. "It's so quiet," she said with a yawn.

Ariadne was already up, and she was leaning on the windowsill, brushing her hair. "Can you hear that?"

"Hear what?" I said, swinging my legs out. The fireplace didn't seem so draughty in the morning sun.

"Birds singing," she said with a grin. "Actual singing! Not just cawing and squawking! There must be lots of different birds around here."

Reluctantly I got out of the bed and opened up my suitcase. I pulled one of the dresses from it and held it up against myself. It was a bit odd to have to wear Ivy's clothes, even if she was my twin. I made a mental note to ask Aunt Sara if she could make me something.

Soon all three of us were dressed, but Rose was still lying in the other four-poster bed. She was awake, but she didn't seem to want to move.

"Are you coming down for breakfast, Rose?" Ariadne asked.

Rose shook her head, but she was smiling. "I like it here," she said quietly. Which I thought was a little odd, but then everything about her was.

"I'll bring you some toast," said Ariadne.

"If there's toast," I said, "I might actually jump for joy."

There was toast. I didn't quite jump for joy, but I did shout "Yes!", earning myself a telling-off from Miss Bowler. She asked where "whatsername" was, and we told her Rose was still resting.

The Shady Pines dining room was big, with huge windows looking over the lake. Everyone from Rookwood was wandering in and finding somewhere to sit, with the teachers presiding over us to make sure we didn't do anything disruptive (like yelling with excitement). There were other guests too, though not many. The tables weren't in long rows like at Rookwood, but arranged in little clusters. Each one had four chairs round it, and was laid out with toast and marmalade and jam. You could order boiled eggs and kippers and, most importantly, there wasn't any gloopy grey porridge in sight.

"This is wonderful," Ariadne sighed. "A proper breakfast."

I spread my toast with strawberry jam and tucked in gleefully, but my mind was elsewhere. Mrs Rudge was running around beside the serving girl, making sure everyone had their food, but besides seeming a bit flustered, she didn't look terrified any more.

I realised that I hadn't told Ivy and the others what I'd seen, and I suddenly felt dreadful. We'd promised no more secrets. I hadn't really been keeping it a secret, I suppose, but I'd still forgotten to tell them.

"Psst," I hissed. I gestured at Ivy and Ariadne to lean in. "I woke up last night, and I saw Mrs Rudge in the corridor. She was acting funny and staring at this cross on the wall."

"That is odd," said Ariadne, peering at the hotel owner without any sort of discretion. "I didn't see any crosses."

"Excuse me," said a voice, and we all jumped back.

The voice belonged to a woman. She was tall, blonde and pretty, wearing a dark long-sleeved blouse and rolled-up trousers, and there was a cap on top of her perfectly curled hair. She looked like she was about to go hiking.

"Phyllis Moss," she said. "How do you do?" She shook

all of our hands and, slightly puzzled, we gave her our names. "I couldn't help noticing that you have a spare seat at your table. May I sit with you all?"

I was about to ask why she didn't just sit at her own table, but Ariadne beat me to it with a friendly smile. "Of course! I don't think our friend is coming down."

"Wonderful," the woman replied, taking the seat. She looked over at me, and then answered my question as if she had read my mind. "My husband has gone out early, you see. He's an ornithologist. That's—"

"Someone who studies birds!" Ariadne piped up.

"Precisely! He says there's all kinds of rare species around here. He's such a bore about it, honestly," she said with a good-natured laugh. "I couldn't stop him heading out at six am with the binoculars."

We all sat there for a moment, unsure quite what to say.

"...toast?" said Ivy, pushing the rack over to Phyllis.

"Ooh, lovely," she said. She picked up a piece and began spreading butter on it daintily. I didn't think I'd ever seen butter spread daintily before. My efforts usually ended in torn toast.

"So you girls are on a school trip?" Phyllis said, reaching for the marmalade. "This is a bit of an unusual destination, isn't it?"

"Our headmistress thinks we need to get to grips with nature," I said, rolling my eyes.

"Yes," Ivy chimed in. "She wants us to do lots of activities, apparently."

"Well, that's a good idea!" Phyllis said cheerily. "You never know when it might come in handy. I actually teach orienteering skills myself. Who's your headmistress? I might offer my services..."

"The lady over there with the glasses, who looks constantly enthusiastic," I said, pointing at Mrs Knight – although now I thought about it, Phyllis Moss looked like she had plenty of enthusiasm to share too.

"Oh, here's my husband!" She suddenly stood up and waved him over. "Julian, this is Scarlet, Ivy and Ariadne."

The man came over and put his arm round his wife. He was wearing a grey tweed suit-jacket and trousers that were muddy at the knees, and a pair of binoculars hung round his neck.

"Charmed," he said shyly, pushing his glasses up his nose. "How's my lovely wife?"

"Well, I was a little lonely having breakfast by myself," she said, giving him a playful jab.

"Those peregrines won't watch themselves," Julian teased back. These two were sickening.

"But," she continued, "the girls' friend hasn't come down

for breakfast, so they let me sit with them. They've just told me that their headmistress wants to do some nature activities here. So I might be able to help out."

"Sounds wonderful, darling. I must be off again, though." He picked up a slice of dry toast. "I want to see if I can spot a pied flycatcher."

"Oh, all right." Phyllis pouted a little and reluctantly let him disappear from the dining hall. She sat down again and finished her toast, then wiped the crumbs from her cheeks. "I'm going to have a little chat with your headmistress and see if we can arrange something fun. Lovely to meet you!" She headed off in the direction of Mrs Knight.

"She seemed nice," said Ariadne.

"If you like people who are totally insipid," I said, and Ivy whacked me with a napkin. I hoped I could finish my breakfast in peace now.

And that was when Cassandra walked in and screeched: "WHO'S BEEN GOING THROUGH MY THINGS?"

Chapter Nine

IVY

Everyone in the hall turned to face Cassandra. I'd been raising a cup of tea to my mouth and had almost thrown it in my lap. Why was she so angry?

Miss Bowler stood up and marched towards her. "Miss Clarkson, I hope you have a good reason for shouting like that in front of all these guests? Is the hotel on fire? Is the world ending?"

Cassandra was shaking with rage, and even the threat of Miss Bowler didn't stall her. "Someone's taken my necklace!" Her eyes flicked around the room and then came to settle at our table. Her nostrils flared and she barrelled over. "Was it your weird little friend, hmm?" She whispered angrily in my ear. "Where is she? All her clothes are stolen; she steals our friend's place on the trip; now she wants to steal my jewellery too?"

I was about to say something in retaliation, but Miss Bowler pulled her off me. The teacup wobbled in my hand. "What is the meaning of this? What necklace?"

Cassandra spun round, breathing heavily. "My grand-mother gave me a gold locket on my birthday, Miss. It's a family heirloom, and someone's taken it! They've rifled through mine and Elsie's suitcases and the necklace is gone!" She looked like she was about to burst into tears.

Elsie was in the archway that led into the dining room now, her face red and her arms folded.

"I bet I know who did it," she said darkly.

"Now then, girls," said Mrs Knight, heading over from where she'd been talking with Phyllis Moss, presumably about orienteering. "Let's go to your room and sort this out, shall we? You've probably just misplaced it. We'll have a look round. No more shouting, please." She held her arms out and raised her voice. "Rookwood girls, finish your breakfast, get ready and then we'll meet up at the hotel entrance for our first activity!"

Cassandra leant down by my ear again. "I'll get her for

this," she hissed. Then she marched back out, Mrs Knight shepherding her and Elsie towards the stairs.

I saw other guests shaking their heads in dismay, and slowly a murmur of conversation began to bubble up again.

"What did she say to you?" Scarlet frowned.

"She thinks Rose stole her necklace," I said. I thought that was very unlikely. Violet may have stolen clothes and food for Rose in the past, but Rose herself had never been a thief.

"We don't even know if it's really been stolen!" Her frown deepened. "I don't trust those two."

"Me neither," said Ariadne.

I finally took a sip of the tea. It had gone cold.

We went back to the room after breakfast and found Rose sitting on the bed. She was up and dressed this time, and reading one of the pony books that she'd borrowed from the school library.

"Rose," Scarlet said as we walked in. "I hate to tell you this, but I think you're a wanted criminal."

Rose put the book down. "What?" she said quietly.

"Cassandra and Elsie said someone went through their things and stole a necklace," I explained. "They think it was you, for some reason."

"Violet's fault, I think," Scarlet added, with a little too much glee.

Rose looked horrified.

"Well, we know it wasn't you who stole it, if it was indeed stolen," said Ariadne. "Because you were here all night, and this morning you've just been in here reading, haven't you?"

Rose nodded carefully.

"Not to mention," Scarlet added, kicking her foot against the corner of the bedframe, "that Rose wouldn't steal anything in the first place. Who do those witches think they are?"

We had gone past their room, but the door had been shut, and all we could hear was muffled conversation coming from inside. I wondered if Cassandra's heirloom would be found under a sock or something, and she'd have to say sorry. She didn't seem the type to apologise.

We started getting ready to go out on whatever activity it was Mrs Knight had planned. I didn't own any trousers or walking boots, so I had to make do with some thick woollen stockings and my school shoes. Scarlet wore much the same, while Rose wore a pair of jodhpurs and Ariadne actually had what looked like a full hiking outfit.

"Where did you get those clothes from?" I asked.

Ariadne was unpacking her camera equipment, rolls of film in their black cases and boxes of paper spilling out of the bag. She craned her head up to look at me, and gestured down at herself. "Oh, all this? Daddy bought it for me when I was at my old school. We used to go on nature walks, and he said I had to be prepared for the dangers of the outside world." She sighed. "I'm surprised he didn't send me a safety helmet and a lifejacket when he heard about this trip."

I giggled. I could certainly imagine him doing that.

She pulled the camera strap round her neck. "I can't wait to get started on the photographs. I need to document as much of the trip as possible for Mrs Knight." She grinned, apparently very pleased at her new responsibility.

When we were all dressed, we headed out into the corridor.

"THERE SHE IS!" a voice yelled.

Within moments, Cassandra was bearing down on us. She towered over Rose.

"Did you take it? Did you take my necklace?"

Rose said nothing.

"What's the matter?" Cassandra sneered. "Cat got your tongue? Answer me!"

Elsie peered out of their room and then hurried over. "Cassie," she said, "it's probably just lost. That's what Mrs Knight said." She looked around hurriedly. I had the suspicion that she knew the teachers were nearby, and didn't want to endanger her prefect status.

Cassandra leant in closer, and her eyes glinted. "Look,

she has a gold necklace on, I can see the chain peeking out of her jumper! It's mine, isn't it? Give it back, thief!"

I stepped forward. "That's not yours. It's Rose's. She always wears it!" Scarlet stepped forward too, always ready for a fight.

"It's true," said Ariadne, her chin wobbling. "It is hers."

"Oh, *really*?" The prefect's expression turned more mean than angry. "Then show it to me."

She reached out and tried to grab the chain, but Rose batted her hand away with surprising strength. "No," she said firmly.

I think it was the loudest I'd ever heard Rose speak, and it made Ariadne gasp. Seconds later, Rose was tucking the necklace away inside her jumper and running for the stairs, Cassandra gaping after her. I half wondered why Rose wouldn't show them the locket, but then she didn't owe those two anything.

"That practically proves it! She must be guilty! The little creep..."

Elsie grabbed her arm. "Stop it, Cassie. We're going to be late. And we're supposed to be in charge of these shrimps."

Scarlet glared furiously at them both. "You're not better than us just because you're bigger and older, and a *murderer* gave you a shiny badge. Grow up!"

And with that, my twin stomped away, leaving both of

the prefects with perfectly horrified expressions, and Ariadne and me standing beside them.

Ariadne held up the camera. "Smile?" she said.

Mrs Knight and Miss Bowler were standing in the courtyard in front of the hotel, with a crowd of girls in front of them. The weather was warm but humid, and grey clouds were swimming overhead and threatening rain at any moment.

As we made our way into the crowd, I noticed that there was a third person beside the teachers. It was Phyllis Moss, our breakfast-table invader. There were various boxes at her feet, and a stack of papers.

"Good morning, girls!" Mrs Knight greeted us. We chorused 'good morning's back, although it was a lot quieter than it usually was in the school assembly hall. "We've got quite a treat for you today! We *were* just going to go for a walk in the forest, but Miss Moss here has volunteered to give us some instruction in orienteering! Isn't that wonderful?"

There was some uncertain mumbling. I wasn't sure that everyone knew what orienteering actually was. I had some vague ideas that it involved wandering with a compass, but beyond that I had no idea.

Phyllis stepped forward. "Hello, all! I've prepared a bit of an orienteering experience for you." She smiled nervously. "I didn't have time to set out a proper course with needle punches and all that, but I hope we'll have a jolly good time anyway." She picked up the papers off the ground. "I've borrowed all the maps of the surrounding countryside that the hotel had, so we can split into groups of..." She went up on tiptoes and quickly counted our heads. "About five. So we'll split up and head off around the local area..."

I noticed then that Miss Bowler was looking a bit put out. She had her arms folded and her nose in the air. Had she been the one who was supposed to run the day's activity? "Hmmph," she sniffed. "And how do you know the local area?"

Phyllis looked over at her, and her eyes widened like a puppy. I think Miss Bowler had upset her. "I-I studied the maps yesterday after I arrived. It's my profession, after all. And I was interested, of course." She turned back to the rest of us, her sunny smile returning and the papers waving in her hand. "So I've written out some sheets for each group that list landmarks you have to find on the map. The waterfall, the caves, that sort of thing. You will... oh! Who has the pencils?"

Mrs Knight handed her a small cardboard box that rattled.

"Ah, good! Yes, so you will get a pencil, and you need to

tick off when you've found each one. The first team to get back here will be the winners!"

Nadia's hand shot up. "What do we win?"

Mrs Knight smiled. "You get the satisfaction of knowing that you've done a good job and worked well together as a team."

"That's not a prize," Nadia moaned. There was mass grumbling. Scarlet looked very disappointed.

"Nobody said there was a prize," Miss Bowler snapped. "Now everyone shut up and listen!"

Phyllis held up the map, pulled a compass from the box at her feet and began explaining the basics of navigating. I noticed Ariadne was nodding along as if she knew it all already, which given the amount of reading she did, was quite likely.

When she was finished, the teachers began splitting everyone into groups. I heard Mrs Knight say something about prefects and supervision, and my heart sank. "Oh no..."

"What?" said Scarlet.

But Miss Bowler was already scanning the crowd. She pointed somewhere behind us. "You there! Sparks! Get over here!"

We watched as Elsie trudged towards us like she had weights in her shoes. "Yes, Miss?"

"These four can be a group," she said, waving her hand over Scarlet, Ariadne, Rose and me. "And you can be in charge."

Elsie's mouth stretched into a grin. "Yes, Miss. Of course, Miss."

Chapter Ten

SCARLET

It had been bad enough being stuck with Elsie for two bus rides, let alone having to drag ourselves around a dark forest with her. Especially when her friend had just been such a witch to Rose. But Miss Bowler was on the warpath because Phyllis had taken her limelight, and I didn't feel like arguing on this occasion.

"Does anyone else get the impression Elsie likes being in charge?" I muttered.

Rose tried to shuffle behind me and Ivy, and I didn't blame her.

Phyllis came over and handed Elsie the various bits and pieces she'd been demonstrating, along with a whistle that was apparently supposed to save us if we got lost. "I hope you were paying attention, girls," she said. "Now, I want your group to head down the drive and start by the lake."

"Of course," said Elsie with a smile, but she dropped it as soon as Phyllis had moved on. "Ugh. I don't see why we have to split up."

"Because otherwise we'd all find the landmarks at the same time, which would completely defeat the point?" I said. I'd lost all patience with her already, and we'd only been in a group together for five minutes.

"Shut up," Elsie snapped back.

"OK, everyone!" Mrs Knight called out, waving a map to get our attention. "Try to be back here in three hours for lunch!"

Phyllis stood next to her. "I'll be walking around and keeping an eye on how everyone is doing. Remember, if you get lost, head downhill towards the lake. You should be able to see the hotel and some of the big landmarks from the shore. If you still can't find your way, make sure to leave a trail so others can find you. Use your maps wisely. All right, off we go!" She clapped her hands.

"Right." Elsie shoved the map and compass into my hands. "You lot can lead the way. I'll follow."

"We can do all the work for you, you mean?" I couldn't believe it. She had to be joking.

She just waved a perfect prefect hand at me as if she were the king or something. "Go on," she said with a smirk. It was just like being back in first year, with Violet treating me like a slave.

I dragged the other girls into a little circle away from Elsie. If she wanted to be left out, then fine, we'd leave her out. I wasn't going to waste such a good opportunity to explore somewhere other than Rookwood. "All right," I said. "Who's good at map reading?"

Ariadne raised her hand. "Ooh! Ooh! Me!"

"You don't have to raise your hand, Ariadne, we're not in class." I handed her the map.

Rose reached out and tapped my hand. "Compass?" I asked. She nodded. "OK, Rose can do the compass." I prodded Ivy. "We can tick off the landmarks. And Elsie can go for a nice long walk off a short pier."

"Scarlet," Ivy warned, but I could tell she was amused.

"I want to take photographs of the landmarks as well," Ariadne said, putting the map between her knees for a moment and twiddling the knobs on her camera. "I expect they'll be quite spectacular."

So we wandered off back down the hotel drive in the direction of the lake, just as a fine mist of rain began falling from the sky, almost welcome in the warm weather. Thankfully, Elsie was trailing behind us at a safe distance, and so far hadn't actually opened her mouth.

When we were further down the road, near the crumbling *Pleas enjo your sty* sign, Ivy stopped. "Did you hear that?" she said.

"Hear what?" I hadn't heard anything.

She peered into the bushes. "I thought I heard rustling."

"It was probably a squirrel or a deer," said Ariadne thoughtfully. Her eyes went bright. "Perhaps I could photograph it!"

I grabbed her arm before she could run off into the bushes. "No, Ariadne. Let's stay on track, shall we? We haven't even got to our starting point yet."

We finally reached the lake, which was very different in the daylight. I stopped briefly on the road to take a look. It was amazing even under the grey clouds, shimmering silver like an enormous mirror. The trees surrounded it in an endless sea of green, their branches gently waving in the breeze. It was so quiet and tranquil.

"Hurry up, Grey!" Elsie yelled from behind me.

Well. Perhaps not *that* quiet and tranquil.

Ariadne was studying the map as she walked. "I think we should head for the dam first as it's nearby. And not difficult to spot!" She pointed south, and I saw what she meant. It was a towering structure made of grey stone, topped with huge arches like the battlements of some great fortress.

As we walked closer, the sound of rushing water grew and grew until it was practically a roar. Rose clamped her hands over her ears.

"What is that?" Ivy asked, or more accurately, shouted.

But as the road came up to the edge of the dam, we could see what was happening. Water was cascading from the holes and spilling down the side in an enormous white torrent, spanning the whole width of the lake.

"Gosh," said Ariadne, raising her camera to take a picture. "This is what's holding back all that water!"

Even Elsie looked awestruck. At least for a moment. "Is this one of the things we have to find?" She tried to snatch the piece of paper off me, but I held on to it.

"Yes," I said indignantly.

"Right! Tick it off, then! I want this to be over as soon as possible!"

I held the paper up in the air and tried to draw a tick in the box in the slowest, most sarcastic way I could manage. She glared back at me. Nothing new there.

She stalked round to where Ariadne was taking pictures and grabbed the map off her. "Let's go to the caves," she said. "Come on." Then suddenly she was walking off into the forest, and we had to run after her, the sound of the rushing water fading into the background.

The forest surrounded the lake, and as soon as you got a little way in, the trees began to block out the sun, the light only shining through in pinpricks. The smell of pine filled the air, and the ground was a mass of mud and needles that the trees had dropped, almost like a carpet.

We got quite a way in, all of us staring up in awe at our surroundings.

"Does she even know where we're going?" Ivy asked as we hurried after the prefect, who was striding along as if she owned the forest.

Rose showed Ariadne the compass. "It's roughly the right direction... I think," Ariadne said. "Oh, I wish she'd give the map back!"

I tried to speed up, but seconds later my foot caught on something and I went flying into the mud. I cried out, my hands scraping the ground as I tumbled.

"Scarlet!" Ivy hurried over. "Are you all right?"

"I'm fine," I said, scrambling to my feet. "I just tripped on something." I looked down at myself. *Ugh*. There was mud all up my stockings and pine needles stuck to my sore hands. I brushed them off on my knees.

Ariadne and Rose caught up. "What did you trip on?" Ariadne asked.

I looked down at where I'd fallen, and brushed away a pile of needles. Something cream-coloured shone through. I dug it out, and then I realised what it was.

It was a skull.

"Urrgggh!" I dropped it immediately.

Ivy had gone pale. "I don't like skulls."

Ariadne crouched down, looking fascinated. "I think it's a goat," she said. "Or maybe a sheep."

"It's horrible is what it is," I said, regretting that I'd touched the thing. In school we had a human skeleton named Wilhelmina that I'd used as a genius hiding place, but it was old and clean and white. This was none of those things. "I'm going to wash my hands three times when we get back to the hotel."

Apparently Elsie had heard the commotion and wandered over. "That wasn't very graceful now, was it?" she said, looking me up and down. "I thought you were a ballet dancer?"

I snatched the map off her and handed it to Ariadne. "And I thought you weren't a total idiot, but we can't be right all the time, can we?"

She drew herself up to her full height and stood over me, her arms twitching at her sides. "Right, Grey. Are you asking for a fight?"

"Well, let me tell you—" I started.

"Um," Ariadne said loudly.

I froze, my hand halfway into the air, Elsie looking like she was just about to shove me, and turned to look at Ariadne's anxious face.

"I think we're lost," she said.

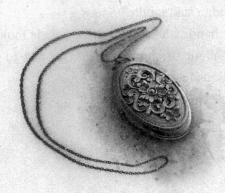

Chapter Eleven

IVY

I peered over my best friend's shoulder at the map.

"What do you mean, we're lost?" Elsie demanded.

"Well, I'm afraid it's your fault," said Ariadne, in what was possibly the politest accusation ever. "I'm not certain if we went in the right direction, and now I don't know exactly where we are."

Rose pointed downhill. "We should go to the lake," she whispered.

I knew what she meant. "Yes, Miss Moss said we should head downhill towards the lake if we got lost."

We all looked around. The land was only very slightly sloping at this point, and I couldn't say for certain which way was downhill. I thought I could hear the rushing of the dam very slightly, but I didn't know which direction it was coming from.

I shivered a little. It was much colder in the shade than it was out in the sunlight, and it suddenly felt like the trees were giants, closing in on us.

And as I listened, I heard it again. A rustling noise, though this time it sounded like footsteps on the carpet of pine needles. This time the others heard it too, and we all looked around.

"Hello?" Scarlet called out. "Is anyone there? Nadia?" she tried. "Anna?"

But there was no answer. I frowned.

"Probably just birds," Elsie snapped. "Now can we please sort out where we're going?"

"This is your fault," Scarlet reminded her.

Before they could start shoving each other, Rose stepped forward and started walking off into the trees. I had no idea if she knew where she was going, but I didn't think it was a good moment to ask. If she had a plan, I was going to follow. The other girls trailed after us, Scarlet and Elsie still bickering.

Rose was moving quickly, but her head was tilted down

– she was looking at something on the ground. Eventually, the forest thinned out a little and she came to a halt in front of a rock face, the rest of us breathless behind her.

"Look," she said quietly.

"The caves!" I exclaimed. "You found them!"

There was a huge black opening in the rock. I went over to it and felt the chill of the shade as I heard the echo of water dripping somewhere deep inside.

"We're not lost, then!" said Scarlet, cheering up a little. Elsie remained unimpressed.

Rose pointed at the ground. Ariadne looked down and said: "Oh! Tracks!"

So Rose had followed the tracks to get here? I could see them, now she'd pointed them out: animal tracks in the mud.

"Looks like a fox, or a badger, maybe," Ariadne continued. She handed the map to Rose and put her camera up to her eye, stalking through the mud to try to get a good picture. "They probably shelter in the caves. Oh!" she said suddenly.

"What?" Scarlet asked.

"There's some people footprints too. Probably some of the others got here first. Perhaps Miss Moss – she said she was going to walk around and..." Ariadne paused for a moment. "Oh..."

"What?" It was me this time.

"I think I'm stuck."

It took quite a lot of tugging to free Ariadne, and she came out without her boot. We managed to dig it out separately, but it didn't look like it would ever be clean again. At least she didn't seem to mind too much.

Eventually we found ourselves back at the lake, having ticked off most of the list on the way: the caves, the waterfall, the stone cairn, the tallest tree (marked with a wooden sign) and the ancient-looking tree split in two by a lightning strike. And of course, Ariadne had photographed all of them. That meant the only thing left to find was the tower.

Once Rose had pointed us in the right direction with the compass and we had found the track that circled the lake once again, the tower wasn't hard to spot. In fact, it was difficult to miss.

It stood proud over the water like something out of a fairy tale. Made of the same dark stone as the dam, it was tall and rounded with pointed turrets, their rooftops made of a greenish copper.

"It looks magical," Ariadne sighed.

"What do you suppose it was built for?" I asked. I wondered if it was a folly, some rich lord's idea of something to impress his beloved.

"I think it was built at the same time as the dam," said Ariadne. "Or at least it looks that way." And she was right, it did. They were a very similar style.

I suddenly had the feeling that we were being watched, but as I turned I found Elsie peering over my shoulder. "I can see the blasted tower," she said. "Cross it off."

"We're supposed to go there," I said. "Or else what's the point?"

"What's the point of any of this?" Elsie's face flushed red.

"Working together as a team?" Ariadne offered.

Elsie narrowed her eyes. "I don't want to work as a team with any of you. You should be doing as I say, or I'll tell Mrs Knight that you didn't behave."

"We rarely do," muttered Scarlet.

"We're going back," said the prefect decisively, "because I'm tired and hungry and I'm fed up with having to traipse around after you lot." Evidently she wasn't feeling the magic of the surroundings. "And I want to help Cassie find her necklace. That is, if it isn't the one round *your* neck." She looked pointedly at Rose.

Rose cowered back, her hand rising protectively, though you could no longer see her necklace at all. She shook her head, over and over.

"Then you'll let me see it, won't you?" Elsie tried again.

She took a step closer, reminding me uncomfortably of a wolf stalking a sheep.

"All right, fine," Scarlet snapped, jumping in front of her. "We'll go back. Just leave Rose alone. How many times do we have to tell you that necklace is hers?"

"Hmph," Elsie said, and turned quickly, her hair whipping past her ears. Then she was striding away – probably in the wrong direction again.

"Well, we can see the tower," I said, reluctantly ticking it off the list. "I suppose that sort of counts." I longed to go near it, to find out what was inside. I imagined a princess brushing her long golden hair out of the top window, or a beanstalk climbing its way up to meet a giant.

I sighed. Life was rarely a fairy tale.

We finally made it back to the hotel courtyard, without getting lost on the way. We sat down heavily on the gravel, back to back. My stomach was growling, my clothes were sticking to me and my feet ached from all the walking.

And to make things worse, we weren't the first to get back – we had been beaten by Cassandra's group.

"Good job, Cassie," Elsie had said cheerfully as she ran over to her, obviously relishing the chance to get away from us.

"She probably cheated," Scarlet whispered.

Phyllis congratulated us on ticking off our whole list, though I felt a little guilty about the tower.

When everyone else had returned, in various states of muddiness and exhaustion, Mrs Knight ordered us all to go and get changed into clean clothes and then head down to the restaurant for lunch. Apparently the hotel had prepared everyone sandwiches. My mouth watered at the thought.

But when we'd all changed and walked back downstairs, we found Mrs Rudge hastily shutting the doors of the restaurant.

"The restaurant is closed," she said hurriedly.

"But Mrs Knight said there would be sandwiches," Scarlet told her, looking distraught. I knew how she felt. "What's changed?"

"Erm..." Mrs Rudge leant back against the door. "One of the staff has suddenly fallen ill. It's best if nobody goes in for the time being. You can eat the sandwiches outside," she said. "I'll bring them to you. Lovely weather today. Won't that be nice?"

It wasn't *that* lovely. In fact, it was muggy and occasionally drizzly, and I felt I'd had enough of the outdoors. But I was ravenous by that point, and decided I didn't mind where we went as long as it involved food.

As we traipsed back outside, Ariadne muttered: "Well, that was strange."

"Indeed," said Scarlet. "She's an odd one, that woman."

I agreed. There was a lot odd about this place. But for the moment, I was still just relieved that it wasn't Rookwood.

Chapter Twelve

SCARLET

Mrs Rudge may have been acting weirdly, but Mr Rudge was even weirder. We hadn't seen him since the first night, when he'd been spectacularly grumpy, but that evening he was prowling around the hotel like some sort of big cat. He kept glaring at everyone, eyeing us with suspicion.

He stopped me in the corridor when I was heading for the lavatories. "Up to mischief, are we?" he said.

"No more than usual," I replied, but he didn't seem to hear me.

He was frowning at the wall, his grey brows knitted, and I noticed that the gold cross seemed to have disappeared again. "Mark my words, letting children come here was a bad idea. Bound to be up to something."

"Who are you talking to?" I called after him as he shuffled away, but there was no reply.

Rose still seemed a little nervous after the events of the day. She'd been coming out of her shell recently, but now she'd gone back to being silent again. If I talked to her she would smile, and sometimes even mime a response, but she couldn't seem to bring herself to say anything. She kept nervously patting her jumper as if checking that her necklace was still there – I guessed because she was worried that Cassandra was going to storm in and snatch it off her, but unless Cassandra could turn invisible, she hadn't been anywhere near Rose since that morning.

The other thing that was weird was that Anna Santos had turned up for dinner claiming that someone had been through her things too, and maybe those of the other girls sharing her room. Everything had looked "ruffled", she said. Mrs Knight just blamed their messy packing.

The dinner was marvellous: roast chicken with potatoes and peas, swimming in gravy. The Shady Pines Hotel had its problems, but the cooking wasn't one of them. I was beginning to enjoy myself.

That night I slept better, feeling more accustomed to the strange noises and the draughty fireplace. Or at least, I *was* sleeping better until a clanging alarm bell began to ring, making me shoot bolt upright.

I thought for one horrible moment that I was back at Rookwood again, that the morning bell was going off and I was going to have to go to lessons. But as my bleary eyes got used to the darkness, I remembered where I was. I was in the hotel by the lake, and someone was ringing the fire bell.

I shook Ivy, but she was already awake, and she grabbed my hand in the dark. We hopped out of bed to see that Ariadne had managed to light one of her many candles. Rose had her hands over her ears. I remembered the fire in the library, the billowing smoke and the flames licking through the paper, and felt sudden fear rush through me.

"Where do we go?" Ariadne asked, panicked.

"Outside!" I said, quickly slipping my shoes on without bothering to do up the laces. That was all I could think of. If there was a fire, we needed to get out.

I cracked open the door cautiously, but no smoke poured in. Instead there was just a flurry of other girls bustling out of doors in their nightgowns. We broke out into the stream and followed it down the stairs, which resounded with footsteps.

"Keep going!" I heard Mrs Knight's voice shout from somewhere behind us. She sounded tired. "Everyone out, please! Hurry! No shoving!"

I felt reassured, surrounded by everyone else, with Ivy's hand in mine, but I still expected to see smoke at every corner. Yet there was none. Where was the fire? In the kitchens? In a fireplace? Had someone dropped a candle? The bell carried on ringing, shrill and angry.

We finally reached the reception area and poured out into the cold night air, under a circle of lamplight. Relief washed over me. We were safe. Ivy leant against my shoulder, and I could feel the goosebumps on her arms.

Moments later, Mrs Knight and Miss Bowler appeared in the doorway, having herded everyone outside. Mrs Knight was wearing a blue dressing gown with flowers on it, while Miss Bowler (to my amusement) was wearing a sort of frilly pink nightdress. I had never seen anything more unlikely.

"Line up!" she bellowed over the noise of the ringing bell, acting like we were back at school – although the nightdress definitely took away from the effect. "Everyone STAY CALM!"

I think that made all of us jump, which didn't help.

And then, as we were sleepily shuffling into a line, the bell stopped. Suddenly the valley was silent again.

"Has the fire gone out?" Ivy asked anxiously.

"That or it's got to whoever was ringing the bell..." I said. I didn't really want to think about that.

Now all of us from Rookwood were lined up, I could see that a bunch of the other guests were gathered on the opposite side of the porch. Phyllis was there, with a group of other women. There was a man wearing a very ugly green suit (why was he dressed at this time of night?) and furtively smoking a cigar. An elegant woman in a wheelchair with a silk nightgown glared at him and moved herself out of the way. I wondered if his cigars had been responsible for the fire.

"I can't see any smoke," said Ariadne, looking up at the building. "Perhaps it was only a small one." Rose was peering around frantically, but if she was looking for smoke, she didn't spot it either.

"Where's—" Ivy started, but she was interrupted by Mr and Mrs Rudge suddenly stepping outside.

"Nobody panic," Mrs Rudge said. "Everything is all right. We were merely having a safety exercise. We..."

We all looked at each other, as if to say: *Really? A safety exercise? In the middle of the night?* It didn't seem likely.

"A safety exercise?" the green-suited man shouted,

brandishing the cigar. "It's one in the morning, madam! What were you thinking?"

Mr Rudge stepped up to him. "Don't you talk that way to my wife! I'll have you know it's a very important procedure. We have to make sure everyone can evacuate on time. At night. Mmhmm. When it's dark."

"Pah," said the man, shaking his head. "Ridiculous. *Ridiculous*. I've a good mind to ask for my money back."

"*Well*," Mr Rudge sneered at him, "I can tell you now, you won't be getting it!"

"Gentlemen, please," Mrs Knight called, trotting over to them. "Let's calm down." I think she thought they were about to punch each other, which I'd rather been looking forward to. She turned to Mr Rudge. "Are you saying it's safe to go inside? I was about to take a register..."

Mr Rudge didn't take his eyes off the green-suited man, but instead just waved a hand in the direction of the building. "Yes, yes, it's fine."

Mrs Rudge evidently decided this was a good time to take over. "Well done on getting outside, everyone. Time to go back in. We don't want any of you to freeze!"

"All right, then," said Mrs Knight, though she looked as puzzled as I felt.

I rubbed my head. I still felt like I wasn't quite awake, and that this was all some sort of strange dream. Probably from eating real food instead of just stew. My body wasn't used to it.

"Really?" said Ivy as we traipsed inside, rubbing our arms to get some warmth back. "Couldn't they have at least done that during the day?"

"That would make too much sense," I said sarcastically. So far, very little of what went on at this hotel made sense.

The next morning, I felt myself having to fight to wake up: like I was swimming against a current that tried to drag me down. But I eventually surfaced, blinked in the bright sunlight, and noticed something.

My suitcase had moved.

I climbed out of bed, a good deal more sluggishly than I had done in the night, and peered down at it.

I knew it had moved, because I'd tossed it down haphazardly when I was getting ready for bed, and someone had put it back neatly with the clasps shut.

"Ivy?" I said, turning to look at my twin, who was half buried in sheets. "Did you tidy my suitcase?"

"Mm... no?" came the muffled reply.

Ariadne wandered over. "I think someone's touched mine and Rose's suitcases too," she said, pointing at their side of the room, where Rose was staring into her luggage. "They look... how was it Anna put it? 'Ruffled.'" She wrinkled her nose. "I'd barely notice it, but they knocked one of the candles out, and the lens cap from my camera was under the bed, and I *know* I didn't leave it there."

"Did they take anything?" I knelt down and flipped through my belongings, but nothing seemed to be missing.

"I don't think so," said Ariadne. "Unless they took some sweets or candles, because I'm not certain how many of those there were…"

Ivy rolled over. "Someone's going through people's things?" she mumbled. "In the night?"

I snapped my fingers. "The fire alarm! It wasn't a safety exercise or whatever nonsense the Rudges came out with. It was a distraction. For the thief."

"The funny thing is," Ariadne pointed out, "that they don't actually seem to be a thief. The only thing that's been taken is Cassandra Clarkson's necklace, and she might just have lost that."

I remembered the gold cross appearing in the night and Mrs Rudge's horrified expression, and I suddenly felt a chill. Could it be something more sinister than just someone out to steal things?

We went for breakfast, passing several other yawning girls on the way down the staircase. Nobody had enjoyed the rude awakening.

As I queued up to get a boiled egg from the counter, I heard the serving girls muttering to one another as they worked. I leant in so I could hear them better.

"...all that commotion yesterday over a candlestick," the smaller one said, wiping her hands on her apron. "It was just a *candlestick*. I put it out on the table because I thought it looked pretty. I didn't know Mrs Rudge was going to go spare."

The larger one nodded. "These city folk are madder than a box of frogs. It looked ordinary to me. Pr'haps a bit old. Maybe it was pricey, but still. She didn't have to shut the dining room."

As soon as they noticed me standing there, the conversation came to an abrupt halt, and I was handed an egg.

I went back to our table and told the others what I'd just heard. Ivy frowned, Ariadne looked puzzled and Rose seemed uninterested – probably because she was getting a proper breakfast for what might be the first time ever. She seemed to be enjoying her toast immensely.

"So we couldn't have our sandwiches inside because someone put a candlestick out?" Ivy wrinkled her nose. "That's ridiculous."

Ariadne was staring into the distance as she often did when she was thinking. "So we have Mrs Rudge getting horribly frightened by a cross and perhaps a candlestick, and people's possessions moving in the night."

I thought about it. "And I heard strange noises, and that draught of cold air from the fireplace... You don't think..." I took a deep breath. It was probably crazy, but... "You don't think that perhaps... this hotel is *haunted*?"

Chapter Thirteen

IVY

I thought Scarlet was perhaps taking things a bit far. Maybe there were such things as ghosts, and the hotel certainly was strange – but why would it be haunted? I said as much to my twin, and she simply shrugged.

"Perhaps not. But you've got to admit it's all weird," she said. And it was true.

We'd only just finished breakfast when I saw Elsie heading towards us from the other side of the room.

"Here comes trouble," I said.

"Oh, for goodness' sake," muttered Scarlet. "Why can't she leave us alone?"

When Elsie reached us she leant over, putting her hands on the tablecloth. "Some of the girls have been telling me that someone has been going through their things. You wouldn't happen to know anything about that, would you?" She stared pointedly at Rose, who leant back in her chair about as far as she could.

"No," said Scarlet. "Because someone went through *our* things as well."

Elsie evidently hadn't expected that development, because she stood up straight again. "Oh?"

"She's telling the truth," I added. "And Rose has been with us the whole time." Ariadne nodded in agreement, taking Rose's hand.

"Hmmph," was all the prefect said, before scuttling to the next table to interrogate the girls there.

"I'm going to kill her if she accuses Rose one more time," Scarlet said.

I gave my twin a look. She said terrible things sometimes. "I wouldn't do that," I cautioned. "I bet Elsie would haunt you out of sheer pig-headedness."

That morning, we were meant to go out into the courtyard to meet again, but the drizzle had turned to heavier rain, and Miss Bowler decided to tell us the day's activity in the reception area instead. She had already ordered us at lunch to put on our oldest clothes that we wouldn't mind getting ruined.

"Right!" she said, as we crowded round her. "Time for a PROPER adventure today, girls! None of this pansy *looking at landmarks*!"

My heart sank. Anything Miss Bowler thought was great was *bound* to be terrible.

"Today we'll be going caving!" she announced – to very little reaction.

"What's that?" said Anna, in her usual slightly baffled tone of voice. "Just going in caves?"

"Quiet, Santos!" Miss Bowler boomed. "Yes, we're going in the caves. For some proper exploring. Now..." she dragged a large chest into view and then banged on the lid. "I've brought some safety equipment. Very important."

She opened the chest up with a creak, and as we craned our necks to peer in, I saw that it was full of helmets. They looked old, most of them a bluish-grey colour but some of them army green, all battered and dented and splattered with dirt.

"Right! Line up! Everyone get a helmet!" She picked up one of her own from a nearby chair – hers had a lamp on the front, I noticed, and looked considerably better quality.

Queuing for the helmets reminded me of the ice skating in winter – the ice skates certainly hadn't been wonderful either, and that "fun activity" hadn't gone well. I felt a horrible sense of foreboding. It wasn't made any better by the fact that the helmet Miss Bowler handed me appeared to have a crack in it, as if someone had whacked it with a rock.

Scarlet fared a little better, with a helmet that at least didn't look damaged even though it wasn't clean. Ariadne's was far too big and wobbled, while Rose's chin strap was too tight and she had to leave it undone.

"Where does Miss Bowler get these things?" I whispered to Ariadne, who just shrugged. I imagined her rifling through rubbish tips, just looking for awful sports equipment that she could force on unsuspecting pupils.

Once everyone was wearing a helmet, Miss Bowler handed out a few torches, then stood up tall and assessed us all. "Let's head out, then, you lot!" she said, looking unusually enthusiastic.

"Is Mrs Knight coming?" Ariadne asked.

"Not today," said Miss Bowler. "She's planning the rest of the week for you. Come on, then, no more questions – let's get going!"

* * *

We trekked through the forest once again, and soon we were at the caves that we'd seen the day before. We saw the same wide, dark mouths in the cliff face, but there was a difference – this time, there was a man with an axe.

Fortunately he was in fact only chopping firewood with it. He looked up as we approached, axe paused in mid-swing. "Whoa there," he called out in a gruff local accent. "Who are you? What are you doing here?"

The man was fairly old, with grey hair and a bushy moustache, and he was dressed like a farmer. His face looked weathered, as if years of sun and rain and snow had found their way into the cracks. He also didn't look very pleased to see us.

Miss Bowler strode up to him. "We've come to see the caves, my good man! These are my students." She gestured at us.

His frown didn't shift. "Haven't seen you around before." He sighed. "You'll be from the hotel, then, I take it?"

"Yes, indeed," Miss Bowler said, and I detected a flicker of annoyance in the man's face.

"Right, right..." He dropped the axe into the mud. "But you're interested in the surroundings? In local history?"

"Of course! Aren't we, girls?" She looked at us sharply, implying that there was a right answer to this question.

"Yes, Miss," we chorused.

That seemed to brighten his mood a little. "Oh, good, good." He nodded to himself. "Most people aren't, see. They just want a pretty view while they eat their fancy meals." He shook his head sadly and then wandered over to one of the trees. "If you're going into the caves, you'll be wanting a guide. It's not safe to go in if you don't know the place."

"That would be jolly good!" Miss Bowler boomed. "Lead the way, then! I'll bring up the rear."

A ghost of a smile lingered on the man's face, and then he went over to a hollow tree trunk, his movements sprightlier than I would have expected. He reached inside the tree, and with wrinkled fingers pulled out a leather bag. From the bag he produced a leather helmet and a stick with a cotton-wrapped end, along with a book of matches. A hat fell out on to the ground, but he tucked it away again. "Follow me, then," he said. "Stay close, and do exactly as I say."

"Yes, sir," everyone said, which made the man look a bit uncomfortable. He probably wasn't used to groups of schoolgirls turning up in this wilderness.

"What's your name, sir?" Ariadne asked. "My name's Ariadne. Like in 'Theseus and the Minotaur'." A few people giggled at this, but it didn't seem to bother her. She always introduced herself that way.

"Mm? Oh, I'm Bob Owens," he said. "You lot can call

me Bob. But no more of that saying things all at the same time." He waved his hand emphatically. "Come on, then." He struck a match and lit the end of the stick, and I realised then what it was.

"A flaming torch!" I gasped aloud.

"That's a bit *medieval*, isn't it?" Miss Bowler said, lighting the flashlight on her superior helmet.

"It gets the job done," Bob muttered. He looked a bit miffed, but he carried on anyway. He headed towards the caves, and we followed.

Scarlet grabbed my hand. "I'm not a fan of confined spaces," she whispered. I understood, images of the asylum flashing in my mind, and I held her hand tight.

The ceiling inside the cave was still head height, even for Bob and Miss Bowler. The green of the forest crept in across the damp stone floor, and stalactites hung from the roof like stone icicles.

"They look pointy," said Ariadne. "I hope they don't fall on our heads."

Rose giggled, but the thought worried me a little. Especially with my not-very-safe safety helmet.

At the back of the cave there was a thin passageway, leading off into pitch-black darkness. Bob went straight over to it. "This way," he said. "Watch your heads. And your feet. Just... just watch everything."

As we followed him, one by one in the flickering torchlight, I saw what he meant. The passageway started off fairly wide, but soon turned into little more than a crack in the rock. I felt Scarlet's hand squeezing my own. "It's all right," I said, trying to be braver than I felt. "He knows what he's doing." I had no idea if he actually did, but that seemed to be a good and reassuring thing to say.

I pushed my way through the crack, having to turn sideways, feeling cold, slimy rock against my skin.

"Yeuuch," I heard Scarlet say behind me. "This is horrible. I want to go back to ballet."

"I think it's fascinating," said Ariadne brightly, and her voice echoed off the walls.

We kept moving forward, sticking close to the person in front of us (in my case, that was Nadia) and behind us (Scarlet). It got colder and colder and darker and darker the further in we went.

"Why can't we *all* have a torch," Scarlet moaned. "I can't see a thing." Then she yelped, suddenly.

"What?" I turned my head, because that was about as much of me as I could turn. But I soon realised what had happened when an icy-cold drop of water splashed on my head, and I yelped too, making her laugh.

"You're going to need to duck here," I heard Bob say from somewhere in the darkness up ahead. "Pass it on."

The message passed down the line. "Why do I need a duck?" Ariadne said.

I soon saw what Bob was talking about as Nadia (moaning about how dirty her clothes were going to get) crouched down on her hands and knees. I reached out and felt the cave wall in front of me – it went down very low, and there was no way I could walk under it. Reluctantly, I let go of Scarlet's hand and crouched down myself. My hands slipped on the freezing floor, and all I could think was that tonnes of rock were just inches above my head, waiting to fall on me.

But then... then I was out the other side, and I could just about stand up again, and the space had widened into a cavern. I could see Bob and the other girls in the orange glow of the flaming torch.

"I can't do it," I heard Scarlet call from the other side.

I put my hands to my mouth. "You can! Just don't think about it!"

"I am thinking about it! That's the problem!" Her voice bounced off the walls.

"It'll be all right, I promise!" I called back.

There was silence, then, and I waited... until I heard shuffling, and eventually Scarlet materialised on all fours, her eyes squeezed tightly shut.

"You did it!" I said.

"I did it?" She opened one eye, then slowly stood up and brushed herself off. "Of course," she said. "Nothing to it."

Not long after, Ariadne appeared, followed by Rose, and then the others. Finally Miss Bowler came huffing and puffing behind them. "Right," she said loudly between gasps, leaning on her knees. "Are we all here?"

"Keep it down a little," Bob said, frowning. "You don't want to set off a rock fall."

"Sorry," Miss Bowler replied in a whisper that was almost as loud as her normal speaking voice. "Time to head down further, then?"

"Not down," said Bob, holding his torch below his face to illuminate a creepy grin. "*Up.*"

Chapter Fourteen

SCARLET

I decided quite quickly that I didn't like caving. It was dark and wet and cold and, worst of all, claustrophobic.

And so far, at least, it had been *dull*. Nothing but rocks to look at. But then Bob got us all to climb up, one by one, through a hole in the roof, and things became a lot more interesting.

The cave opened out into a wide bowl shape, with the hole we had climbed through in the bottom — a bit like a giant sink. With the torches held up, we could see that the roof was covered in pointy stalactites and crystals. The light bounced off them, shimmering prettily.

"Oooh," Ariadne said when she saw it. "If only my camera would work down here." Rose stared upwards in awe.

We all sat round the edge, on the cold sloping stone, in a circle.

"They call this the Devil's Basin," said Bob in a low voice. "Legend has it that a giant witch used this as her cauldron, and the smoke from the magic potions rose up and left the crystals on the roof."

"What balderdash," Miss Bowler guffawed, attempting to clamber out of the hole, but having some difficulty. Bob glared at her, and she quickly changed the subject. "Big girls! Don't just stand there staring! Help me up, will you?"

I tried not to laugh as Elsie and Cassandra, along with a couple of the other prefects, hauled Miss Bowler up and on to the edge. "Oof," she said.

"If you're all quite finished," said Bob haughtily, "it's time for a story. Put your torches out."

"Oh no," I muttered. I didn't want it to be any darker than it already was. I wouldn't be able to see the rock, and it already felt as if it was pressing down on me. My chest tightened.

"Will that be necessary—" Miss Bowler started, but Bob silenced her with another look.

"*Torches out*," he insisted. He put out the one he was carrying, and the smell of smoke filled the air. One by one, the battery-powered torches were turned off, until Miss Bowler finally sighed and reluctantly switched off the one on her helmet.

I gasped. The pitch darkness was suddenly everywhere. Normally at night you had at least the moon and the stars to see by if you didn't have a candle, but this was different. Beneath the earth, the darkness was *real*.

Ivy squeezed my hand beside me. "Take deep breaths," she whispered.

I breathed slowly, in and out, in and out. For a moment, the sound of breathing was all I could hear, and I focused on it. Then Bob began to speak.

"For as long as there have been people in this valley," he started, his voice lowered to the point that I had to lean in to hear him better, "there has been a village. It started as sticks and mud, but it grew over the years to stone and slate. There was a church, and a grocer, and a school. It was never a town, mind, just a village, but the people loved it and cared for it. Generations were raised there, father and son ploughing the fields, cutting peat on the moors, fishing in the river..."

He seemed to get lost in thought for a moment.

"Is there a point to this?" I heard Nadia whisper on my right, and I whacked her on the leg.

"Shush, I want to hear," I said. Concentrating on Bob's words was helping me forget my urge to panic and run away as fast as possible.

"Seren village," he said, "was more than the stone and slate it was built of. It was a home. A place where people belonged."

"I didn't see any villages," said Elsie, and this time lots of people shushed her.

"But one day," Bob continued, as if nobody had interrupted, "a man came to Seren. And he knocked on every door, and he told them that their houses had been bought, that they were no longer their own." He sighed deeply, regretfully. "The city, he said, the big city miles and miles from here, needed the water. And so the people had to leave."

"They didn't have a choice?" Ariadne asked, sounding a little horrified.

"No," he said. "They weren't given one. They had been bought and sold. The valley was to be flooded to make a reservoir. Not even for the locals, no. The water was all going to be pumped away." I could hear a scratching noise then, and I wondered if he was scratching the rock or grinding his teeth. "So they started constructing the dam. A huge, ugly thing that squatted over the valley. People died, they did, building that thing, and they said it was cursed. But they carried on anyway. And soon, the water was rising and rising and the village was under water. Lost forever."

A question was burning on my tongue, and I couldn't hold it any longer. "What happened to the people?"

There was another moment of silence before Bob answered.

"The city men built them new houses, over the hill. But those places are nothing but brick shells, row after row. Their old homes had been destroyed before the lake had even been filled, to make sure they couldn't go back to them. Most of the young folk moved away south. There's barely a man left now."

I shuddered. Those poor people. How could anyone do this?

He took a deep breath. "But it didn't end there. Because all the souls of Seren were buried in the churchyard, all those people who'd had the hills in their bones. And now their bones were trapped under gallons of water, and they couldn't reach the heavens."

His words swirled around us in the darkness, and I felt shivers go down my spine.

"The souls couldn't rest, see. Now they were troubled. And they say... they say that the ghosts of those who are buried haunt the valley. They say," he said, and his voice got even quieter so we had to lean in even closer, "that if you pay close attention late at night... you can hear the ringing of the church bells, and feel the chill of the souls as they pass you by, and see the lights under the lake..."

More moments passed in silence, and I could tell everyone was holding their breath. Then, almost at the edge of hearing, a voice whispered: "*Save us...*"

"Oh my word," Ivy said, and she gripped my hand even tighter.

"Did you hear that?" So much for breathing calmly – now I was sucking huge, cold gulps of air into my lungs.

"I think I heard it," said Ariadne.

And suddenly everyone was talking at once, everyone asking everyone else if they'd heard the voice, and debating what it had said.

"Quiet!" Miss Bowler snapped eventually. "Shut up, the lot of you! Are you quite finished scaring the knickers off them with your mumbo-jumbo ghost stories, Mr Owens?" She flicked her torch back on, and the sudden bright light hurt my eyes, though I was relieved to be able to see again.

"Hmmph," said Bob, but he seemed to be smiling beneath his annoyance.

"Weren't you scared, Miss?" asked Nadia cheekily.

"Not one bit. What a load of tosh." Miss Bowler's hand was shaking. Nobody mentioned it. "Let's get back down."

Once we'd climbed out of the Devil's Basin, which was easier said than done, Bob wanted to go on a little further. "There's one more chamber this way," he said, relighting his torch. "And it's a good one."

Miss Bowler was still in a grump, but she reluctantly agreed. "Then we must get back," she said.

Where had that voice come from? It had sounded so otherworldly and strange. I rubbed my arms, trying to make the goosebumps go away.

We pressed on to the next cave, through a long tunnel that was much less of a squeeze than the way in had been. As we got nearer, I heard a whispering, rushing sound.

"What is that?" Ivy whispered.

But when the tunnel opened out... everyone gasped.

This cave was big and wide, and there were two waterfalls tumbling down from the roof into a pool that stretched out towards the back of the cave, further than I could see.

"Worth it, eh?" said Bob with a grin.

Everyone agreed. Even Rose nodded enthusiastically.

"Lovely," said Miss Bowler, in a way that implied she saw sights like this every day and was thoroughly sick and tired of them. "Right, all, time to head back! Quick sharp! No lollygagging!"

It was easier leaving the cave than getting in, but I still didn't enjoy crawling through the horrible small space. My hands were black with dirt and my clothes were soaked through.

"Thanks, then, Mr... Bob," said Miss Bowler when we were safely out in the open again. She pumped his hand vigorously.

"It's Owens," he said politely, brushing his hands on his overalls.

"Right, right. Come on, then, girls, back to the hotel." Miss Bowler was striding off before we had a chance to protest. Quickly, everyone thanked Mr Owens before following her. I turned back and saw him standing there, his hands in his pockets, just staring off into the forest.

"I've just realised something," said Ariadne as we walked down towards the hotel. We were up on the hillside, and you could glimpse the lake through the trees. She'd stopped for a moment, and was staring at it. "I think I saw those lights under the lake. On the way here."

"I remember that." I shuddered a little. Near the tower, she'd said.

"But there's something else." She frowned, and bit her lip.

"What?" said Ivy.

"Those things that appeared in the hotel, that Mr and Mrs Rudge seemed really scared of..." She trailed off.

"A gold cross?" I said. "And a candlestick?"

She nodded, and her eyes skimmed over the lake. I thought about the drowned village, and suddenly I realised what Ariadne was thinking.

"Don't they..." she whispered. "Don't they seem like the sort of things you would find in a church?"

Chapter Fifteen

Ivy

I wasn't sure what to think about Ariadne's theory. Were they really items from a church? And if Mr Owens's story was true, and there really was a village under the lake... could it be that items from that church were appearing at the hotel? The thought made my skin prickle, but I wasn't sure I believed it.

We'd only been back in our rooms for a short time when I heard someone yelling in the corridor. I went over and peered out.

"Someone's *taken* my suitcase, Miss!" It was Elsie, and

she was flapping desperately at Miss Bowler. "It's just disappeared!"

"You've probably just pushed it too far under the bed, girl," snapped Miss Bowler. She shoved open the prefects' door and ushered Elsie back inside. "It'll turn up!"

I retreated into our room again. "Elsie's suitcase has disappeared, apparently," I said.

"Nobody cares," said Scarlet, who was changing into clean clothes behind the curtains of the four-poster.

"I know, but isn't it weird? There's things going missing, and things appearing that shouldn't be there..." I'd never been one to believe in hauntings, but there was something going on here, and I had no idea what it was.

"It is spectacularly odd," Ariadne agreed. "I think we need to investigate further—"

She was interrupted by the sound of Rose snoring. As soon as we'd got in, Rose had collapsed on their bed. She'd seemed exhausted from all the walking, and clambering about in caves. I supposed she hadn't walked far in a long time.

We didn't have the heart to wake her for lunch, so we decided we'd bring her up some food. This time the dining hall was actually open, and we all helped ourselves to cheese and ham sandwiches.

Not long afterwards, Phyllis Moss walked in and spotted

us at our table. She hurried over. "Oh, girls! Just the three of you again?"

We nodded. "Our friend is sleeping," I said. "I think she's too tired from all the walking."

"I got her a sandwich," said Ariadne, waving said sandwich in the air.

Phyllis smiled. "Ah," she said. "Well. I was just going to speak to your headmistress again. If the rest of you aren't too tired, Julian has offered to take you all for a spot of birdwatching. Won't that be jolly?"

"Jolly boring," Scarlet muttered, but thankfully Phyllis didn't seem to hear her.

"Sounds wonderful," said Ariadne, a good deal louder.

I just smiled, and carried on munching my sandwich. I was a little tired too, and I hoped I would feel better once I'd eaten.

"See you later," Phyllis said. Her smile was so cheerful that it was infectious. Soon she was off to chat to Mrs Knight once again.

After lunch, we all gathered in the reception area. Mr Rudge was there for a moment, but he looked almost appalled at the sight of us standing around and soon he had disappeared through the door at the back of the room.

"Looks like we have another activity for this afternoon,

everyone!" Mrs Knight called out, wringing her hands together. "We'll be going for a spot of birdwatching with the lovely Mr Moss, as soon as he arrives!"

She said this as if she expected us to jump for joy, although with the possible exception of Ariadne, it was quite the opposite. There was a lot of quiet groaning.

Personally, I was worried about Rose. I didn't want her to wake up and think that we'd abandoned her. We'd left her a sandwich on a tray by the bed, but I decided we ought to tell Mrs Knight she was asleep. I pushed forward through the crowd.

"Mrs Knight?" I tugged gently on her sleeve. She was saying something to Phyllis, who was waiting there, looking at her watch – presumably wondering where her husband had got to.

"Yes, Ivy?" the headmistress said, looking around. I smiled a little, pleased that she'd got the right twin.

"Rose is tired," I said. "She's still asleep, back in the room."

"Ah," said Mrs Knight. Her brow furrowed. "I'm not sure we should leave her on her own."

Phyllis looked up. "I was going to stay here anyway," she said. "Birds are much more Julian's thing than mine. Shall I keep an eye out for her?"

"Oh, would you?" Mrs Knight's expression brightened.

"That would be very kind." I smiled gratefully. At least someone would be there if Rose woke up.

"Don't mention it," Phyllis grinned. "I'll just be rattling about," she continued as I headed back over to Scarlet and Ariadne. "Ah, Julian!"

Mr Moss had walked in, bearing binoculars. He looked a little flustered, and there were leaves in his hair. "Hello, all!" he said with a nervous wave. "Sorry, dear," he said to his wife. "I thought I spotted a merlin and I wanted to sketch it."

Phyllis gave him a withering look, but I could tell she was just pretending. "All right, have fun, you lot..." She strode off towards the corridor.

Julian ran a hand through his dark hair, brushing out some of the leaves. We all stood and watched him expectantly. But for a moment he didn't say a word.

Mrs Knight peered at him. She'd gone a little red in the face. "Mr Moss? The girls are all so excited for your trip today!"

Scarlet yawned.

Julian blinked shyly. "Ah, yes." He smiled. "Sorry. I'm rather more used to birds than people. Let's be off, then, shall we?"

He led us out of the hotel and down the driveway, and then off on a winding path through the trees.

"Where are we going?" I heard someone ask from near the front.

"The bird hide," he explained. "Mr Rudge had it built a few years back. Lots of the guests like to go for a spot of birdwatching, not just myself."

We traipsed through the forest until the path eventually opened out at a wooden hut that was camouflaged with branches and leaves. Julian came to a halt in front of it. "All right," he said. "I'll take a few of you inside at a time. The rest of you, see what you can spot out here." His eyes twinkled and he put a finger to his lips. "And stay quiet. We don't want to scare anything off."

While he took a small group inside, the rest of us waited. Mrs Knight had got a pair of binoculars from somewhere too, and was staring up into the trees and smiling. Miss Bowler was shuffling her feet, looking like she'd much rather be going for a jog.

I crouched down, trying to rest my legs for a moment but not quite wanting to sit on the muddy forest floor. Suddenly someone prodded me with a boot and I nearly toppled forward, but managed to regain my balance.

"Oi!" Scarlet said, forgetting the order to be quiet. "Leave my sister alone!"

I climbed back to my feet and turned to see Cassandra and Elsie, both pulling innocent expressions. I wasn't sure which one of them was responsible, so I just glared at them both.

"Where's your little friend, by the way?" Cassandra asked with a sneer.

"None of your—" Scarlet started, but Ariadne was already answering.

"Back at the hotel," she said.

Cassandra and Elsie shared a look. "So you've left her unattended with all our things?" Cassandra said.

"She's not a thief, Cassandra," I said. "Whatever you may think."

"Of course," Elsie simpered. Then they both giggled and walked away.

Ariadne seemed unbothered by what had just happened. "I still can't see any birds," she said in a low voice, staring around through the viewfinder of her camera. "Well, I might have seen a pigeon."

"I think I just saw a pair of harpies," Scarlet muttered, and I tried not to laugh.

Soon it was our turn to go into the bird hide. It was fairly dark inside, with a couple of benches and a big long slit across one wall, letting in a small amount of light. Julian stood in the corner with his binoculars, peering out. "All right, come and have a look," he said, waving us over.

I sat down on the bench, being careful to avoid any splinters or nails – it was a little crudely made. But then I peered out of the window, and gasped.

The bird hide looked out over a dip in the landscape, just as filled with trees as where we'd come from. But there was something different – someone had strung up bowls filled with seed and sticks of corn. And they were *covered* with birds, of all shapes and sizes. There was even a guilty-looking squirrel hanging from one of the bowls.

"See how many different birds you can spot," Julian whispered. He pointed out robins and nuthatches and greenfinches as he moved along beside the bench. There was a bright yellow bird I didn't think I'd ever seen before, called a siskin. Ariadne looked fascinated, wordlessly snapping away with her camera.

Julian crouched beside me, and I asked him what I was wondering: "Did you put all this up?"

He smiled and shook his head. "No," he said. "This was all Mr Rudge as well. I think he enjoys birdwatching more than he lets on."

That was a funny thought – I wasn't sure I could imagine the humourless hotel owner enjoying anything. "What about your wife – Mrs Moss, I mean?"

There was a flicker of something in his calm expression.

"She's never understood, really. But we both love the great outdoors, so that's something we can share."

Ariadne leant over. "It was very kind of her to stay and look after our friend Rose," she said.

Julian nodded slowly. "Does Rose often stay behind?" He paused, his eyes tracking a blackbird that was hopping through the trees, and then carried on quietly. "Because she wasn't with you at breakfast when I met you, was she?"

I thought about it. "Rose is a bit of a tricky one, I suppose. She does what she likes, really. She doesn't talk much."

Julian put the binoculars to his eyes. "Isn't that a little... strange?"

I didn't know what to say to that. I looked across at Scarlet and Ariadne, who merely shrugged.

"How does she get on at school, if she doesn't talk?" he asked, lowering the binoculars and looking back at me. His eyes were big and blue. "I mean, I had a frightful time at my boarding school just for being different. Old Bird Brain, they used to call me." He shook his head sadly.

"Well, some people pick on her, I suppose."

"And the rest of us," Scarlet added. Which was true, really. People like Penny and Elsie didn't usually discriminate in their horribleness.

"She's not really from our school. She just stays with us," I said.

"Oh," he said, looking puzzled. "Where is she from, then?"

Again I looked at the others, but this time it was because I didn't have an answer at all. "I don't actually know," I said finally. "I don't know anything about her past."

"Hmm," he said, his expression now thoughtful. "That's very odd, isn't it? Haven't there been some thefts and things at the hotel? I mean... do you trust her?"

"Of course," we all said, without even thinking.

But I started to realise that he was right. We didn't really know anything about Rose, or who she was, or where she came from.

And just like that, a tiny speck of doubt crept in.

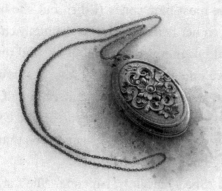

Chapter Sixteen

SCARLET

I wasn't the biggest fan of birdwatching. Birds were pretty, of course, but they didn't do much besides eat and squawk. People-watching was *much* more interesting.

I watched Elsie and Cassandra as they walked back, holding hands and whispering to each other, throwing snide glances at everyone else.

I watched Julian chatting with Mrs Knight and saw her blushing – he was quite handsome, really, and that fact apparently hadn't escaped her.

I watched Nadia and Ethel having a contest to see who

could carry the most pine cones (Ethel, but she balanced some of them on her head, which was definitely cheating).

Ariadne had taken a picture of all of us, and then tried to sneakily take one of Miss Bowler, who was now telling her off and threatening to snap the camera in half.

We were trekking back through the forest, and Ivy turned to me, her eyes worried. "Scarlet... what do you think about what he said? About Rose?"

I shrugged. "She's harmless, isn't she? She's sweet and quiet and she loves pony books. If anyone's not trustworthy, it's those two." I waved at the harpies.

"I suppose," said Ivy. "She is our friend. But he's right that we don't know anything about her. Have we ever even asked?"

I thought about it – I felt sure that I had, but I couldn't think when it had been. "We only know what Violet told us. That she was in the asylum and that her family had her locked up in there because they didn't want her getting the inheritance." I stared down for a moment at the mat of pine needles and twigs that crunched beneath my feet. "Though I don't know if I trust anything that comes out of Violet's mouth," I added.

"We ought to ask her," Ivy said. "If she wants to talk about it, I mean."

"Hmm," I said. "I'd be surprised."

* * *

A bigger surprise was waiting in the hotel. We opened the door to our room to find Rose sitting, open-mouthed, in the middle of chaos.

Our luggage had been tipped out, our clothes strewn all over the floor, Ariadne's camera equipment scattered and Ivy's pearl necklace left hanging from the bed. The curtains were ripped and even the pillows had been tossed across the room, one of them spilling feathers.

I stood in the doorway, the others trying to peer round me. "What on earth?"

Rose turned to look at me, her expression horrified. She shook her head. "I didn't..." she whispered.

I walked in so the others could get past. Ariadne gasped. "Oh, Rose! What happened?"

Rose's mouth flapped open and shut. She just couldn't find the words. For once, I knew how she felt.

"Did someone do this while you were here?" Ivy asked her. "Did you see anything?"

But she simply shook her head, and then sat down heavily on the bed.

"You were asleep when we left," said Ariadne gently, tiptoeing over the spilt rolls of film and putting her camera on the bedside table. "Did you wake up and go somewhere?"

This time Rose nodded. She looked ashamed. Ariadne put an arm round her shoulders.

I just wandered around hopelessly. I picked up my bag and hugged it to my chest. *Why would anyone do this?* I thought. I hated the idea of someone touching my things, just throwing them around as if they didn't matter. And then I thought of Bob's story, and a small voice in the back of my mind said: *What if it wasn't a person?*

"We need to tell Mrs Knight," Ivy said, grabbing my arm before my train of thought could go any further. Reluctantly, I put my bag back down on the floor and followed her out into the corridor.

"You don't think..." she whispered as we hurried along. "That maybe Rose did that?"

I wrinkled my nose. "Why would she?"

Ivy frowned. "I don't know. But she was alone in the room. What if she sleepwalks or something?"

That was a possibility, I had to admit it. But then other people had had their bags rifled through, and that couldn't have been her... could it?

We found Mrs Knight downstairs and told her what had happened.

"Goodness, girls," she said, shaking her head. "Not *again*. Just tidy everything up and make sure nothing's missing. I'll have to go and tell Mr Rudge." She sighed.

"This isn't right, Miss," Ivy said. "Maybe we should go home? Get a refund?"

At that moment, Julian walked by, flashing Mrs Knight a bright smile. She brushed her hands on her dress, looking flustered. "Well, perhaps not just yet, eh? But I'm not sure what else I can do. We'll just have to keep an eye out for any more strange behaviour."

"I think there's a strange behaviour epidemic in this hotel," I said. "And I thought Phyllis was going to keep an eye out for Rose?"

But Mrs Knight ignored me, her eyes still following Julian down the corridor. "Don't worry yourselves, girls. Dinner is at seven, so make sure you're all ready for then," she said. "Off you go!" She waved us off with a little smile.

"Why is she acting like that?" asked Ivy crossly. I could tell she'd hoped that Mrs Knight might actually do something this time.

"She's mooning over Julian," I said. "He makes her giggle like a schoolgirl."

"Ugh," said Ivy. She sounded just like me, and I couldn't help but smile.

We began tidying up the room, Rose doing her best to assist. She still didn't say a word, but she managed to seem apologetic the whole time as she rushed back and forth picking things up.

I watched her closely. What if Ivy was right? What if

Rose was somehow doing strange things without knowing it? She had been in the asylum, after all.

So have you, my mind snapped at me. I sighed, and tried to forget about it.

Moments later, I heard a snort of laughter, and Cassandra was standing in the doorway, arms folded. "I told you so," she said. She smiled at Rose. "She's crazy and a thief."

"Oh, go away, *Cassie*," I said sarcastically as Rose started quivering with nerves. "You're not helping."

"Why don't you ask her where she got that necklace?" Cassandra hissed through her teeth. "Or where she came from? Or why she doesn't talk?" She narrowed her eyes, just like a snake. "Don't come crying to me when she's murdered you all in your sleep." She strode away, her footsteps echoing off the walls.

I was tempted to run after her and give her a good hiding, but Rose's eyes had filled with tears. "Don't cry, Rose," I said. "She isn't worth it. Just ignore her." But I had to admit, I was curious to know the answer to those questions too.

When everything was back in our bags, we all lay down on one of the beds, exhausted. I'd thrown myself on to it and stared up at the torn curtains and the dust motes that floated through the air in the last light of the evening. What did it all mean?

My stomach growled, and I hoped it wouldn't be long until dinner.

And then I heard a quiet voice, and it took me a moment to realise that Rose was speaking.

"My family didn't want me," she said, barely louder than a mouse. "My mother and father passed away, and the others, they... they didn't want me to inherit the estate. They said that I didn't deserve it and they did."

I stayed completely still, not daring to say a word.

"They told everyone I was mad. I think... perhaps even I believed it. They had me put in the asylum. They wanted to take what was mine and then get rid of me, forever."

I felt a pang of sympathy. I was sure our stepmother would do the same.

"My mother gave me this." Rose sat up then, and the rest of us sat up too, to look at her. Wordlessly, she pulled the necklace out from where it was hidden under her clothes, and prised open the locket. She held it out for us to see.

Inside it was a tiny key.

And then, before we could ask what it was, she had closed it up again, and hidden it away once more.

Chapter Seventeen

Ivy

Rose was certainly a mystery, but there was more mystery to come.

I woke early the next morning, while it was still mostly dark, to the sound of water running. I peered sleepily out from the covers to see that the strange bath in the corner of the room was filling up, nearly overflowing.

"Oh my goodness," I said, and quickly hopped out of bed. I ran over and wrenched the tap shut, the water spluttering on to my nightgown. It was a little murky, with pieces of leaf in it.

Scarlet rubbed her eyes and stared at me. "Odd time for a bath, isn't it?"

"I wasn't running it," I said. "It just woke me up." I looked around the room, and realised something: Scarlet, Ariadne and Rose were all still in bed. *So who turned the tap on?*

I yanked the plug out of the bath, watching as the water began to gurgle away. Scarlet yawned and rolled over, apparently no longer interested. But now I felt a chill, and I couldn't shake the feeling that there was someone in the room. I tiptoed around, peering behind the curtains and into the cupboards, but mostly it was too dark to see anything. The draught from the fireplace brushed past my legs and made me shiver.

As I passed Ariadne and Rose's bed – Ariadne snoring softly and Rose lying on her back with her eyes shut tight – I noticed that their sheets were all pushed back, and I wondered for a moment if the sleepwalking theory might have something to it. But Rose looked so peaceful, her golden hair tumbled over her shoulders like Sleeping Beauty.

I tried to tell myself I was being silly, and that nothing

strange was going on. The pipes were probably just faulty. No one had been in our room.

But just in case, I picked up the poker from beside the fireplace, and held on to it as I climbed back into bed.

When I woke again, the sky I glimpsed through the curtains was bright but grey. No one mentioned the bath incident, and I began to wonder if I'd dreamt it. But the poker was lying on the floor next to our bed, and when I peered into the cast-iron tub, I could see pieces of leaf still swimming in the bottom.

I tried to forget about it as we went downstairs for breakfast. Everything seemed normal: Miss Bowler was bellowing at Anna for dropping the kippers, the prefects were bickering about something, and the hotel staff were happily bustling around with jugs of milk and racks of toast.

But things took an even stranger turn when we were walking back up to the room and heard someone shriek.

Scarlet and I ran to the reception area to find Mrs Rudge standing over the desk with her hands clamped over her mouth. There was a bulging, waterlogged book on the desk. It looked ancient, falling to pieces, and it was dripping on to the carpet.

"Are you all right, Miss?" I asked, hurrying over.

Her eyes darted up at us, and she seemed to finally

register that we were there. I was close enough to read the peeling gold lettering on the front of the volume – it was a prayer book.

The chill from the previous night washed over me again, and it brought with it everything that Bob Owens had told us. *The village. The lake. The flooding.*

A picture swam into my head. The church, under the water, lake weeds blowing silently in the current. Silent pews with nothing but fish swimming around them. A silent altar with a golden cross, with candlesticks...

And there would be prayer books. Of course there would.

Mrs Rudge eventually spoke. "Were you looking for something, girls?" she said flatly, her eyes giving nothing away.

"We heard you scream," said Scarlet. "We thought something was wrong."

"You were mistaken," said Mrs Rudge, only the slightest quaver in her voice. "Everything is quite all right."

"But... that?" I said, waving at the sodden book.

The hotel owner blinked down at it as if she'd never seen it before in her life. "I don't..." She seemed to panic for a second, but then she plastered a smile on to her face, like this was all a big joke that we hadn't quite understood. "Oh, well, it's mine. It... was mine when I was a child. I just spilt some water on it, that's all."

I didn't point out that there was no cup or bucket nearby, nothing she could possibly have spilt. She was obviously hiding her horror, and I wanted to know why.

But, as always, Scarlet was quicker to say something than me. "Does this have anything to do with the golden cross from the other night?"

Mrs Rudge's eyes went wide. "I... I had a very religious upbringing," she said, and before we could ask anything else, she had snapped up the wet book and hurried away to the back room.

Scarlet shrugged and headed towards to the corridor.

"Something is very wrong here," I said, following and tugging at her sleeve. "She's lying, isn't she?"

"If she's not lying," said Scarlet, "then I'm the Queen of Sheba."

I tried to think about what it all meant. Because from where I was standing, it seemed like my twin's crazy theory was right, and that items from the sunken church *were* mysteriously appearing at the hotel. And for some reason, the Rudges were trying to pretend it wasn't happening.

And apart from that... what about the bath filling with water? And what had happened to our room, not to mention people's possessions being rifled through and jewellery vanishing? Was it even possible that a vengeful spirit, or even a whole host of the things, was targeting the Shady Pines?

That thought scared me, but I still wasn't sure if I believed it. What was far more likely, and perhaps more worrying, was that this was all the doing of a person. And Scarlet and I knew very well just how dangerous the wrong people could be.

That day's activity, Mrs Knight informed us, was boating on the lake. The hotel apparently owned a little fleet of rowing boats that were left floating out on the water beside the jetty. And this time, Miss Bowler was in charge. Mrs Knight said that she was going to stay back at the hotel and keep an eye on things, and I was grateful to hear it.

We trekked to the lakeside, past a wooden hut and down beside the moored boats, and I yawned and blinked in the sunlight that was slowly burning through the iron clouds. Miss Bowler was dragging a heavy suitcase along behind her.

I didn't like water much. I wasn't the best swimmer, and neither did I have many good memories surrounding it.

Scarlet wasn't a fan either. "They're going to have to pay me to get in a boat," she muttered.

We lined up on the shore, pebbles crunching underfoot. I took a few steps towards the lake, but the water lapped at my feet like it was trying to pull me in, and I jumped back.

Ariadne was snapping photographs of the lake, with the tower on the other side a huge silhouette on the landscape. It didn't take long for Miss Bowler to come marching over.

"Flitworth!" she barked. "Are you planning on taking that device in a *boat*?"

"Yes, Miss." Ariadne's mousy eyes blinked innocently.

I could tell Miss Bowler hadn't expected her to say yes. "I— Well," she spluttered. "Don't. Leave it on the shore."

Ariadne looked horrified. "What if it gets stolen?"

"Who's going to steal it out here?" Miss Bowler spread her arms out wide and slowly turned from side to side. "A sheep?"

I saw Cassandra sniggering at that, but I didn't think it was so funny. After all, someone *had* been stealing things. Though that had been inside the hotel...

"I can't just leave it out here," said Ariadne as Miss Bowler was distracted by Anna trying to catch a fish. "Daddy will kill me if anything happens to it."

"We're in broad daylight," Scarlet pointed out. "If you leave it right here, we'll be able to see if anyone goes near it."

"I *suppose*." Ariadne reluctantly laid down the camera, taking a long time to let go of the strap.

Having chased Anna back into line, Miss Bowler stood in front of us and looked us up and down as if she were a drill sergeant. "Right, you bunch of wimps! You're in my territory now!" She grinned; a fairly horrible sight. "In a moment, you'll all get back into your groups. Then you'll head in there —" she pointed to the hut — "and get changed into *these*."

She flipped open the suitcase, and revealed a pile of Rookwood's hideous swimming costumes.

"Oh joy," Scarlet muttered. I shuddered at the thought of putting one of those horrible things on again.

"Next," the swimming teacher continued, "you will each get in a boat. We'll all row out over there." She swivelled like a shot-putter and pointed to the murky surface of the lake. "And then you'll get swimming!"

"Miss," said Nadia, her arms folded in her usual indignation, "we can't go in there. It's dirty. There's probably fish and things." She wrinkled her nose.

Miss Bowler wasn't having any of it. "Nonsense, Sayani. It's nature. Get used to it." She watched as we reluctantly got back into our groups from the other day, the four of us marshalled by Elsie, who looked as happy about it as ever.

"Right!" Miss Bowler clapped her hands so loudly I half expected the mountains to shake around us. "Into the hut!"

Chapter Eighteen

SCARLET

I wrestled with the ugly swimming costume, which I could have sworn was still damp.

"I was hoping I'd never have to put one of these on ever again," Ivy said with a grimace.

The changing hut was bare, with nothing inside but benches and a heap of threadbare towels. I doubted the hotel guests went swimming very often.

"I bet there's a monster in there," said Ariadne. She was attempting a balancing act of pulling on her costume under a dangling towel. "I'm sure I've heard of it."

"You're thinking of Loch Ness," Ivy pointed out.

"And besides," I said, trying to pin my hair up over my head, "how would it have got here? This lake is practically new. They poured water on a village."

"You never know with monsters," Ariadne said darkly.

I plonked myself down on one of the benches and looked around. The prefects had all pulled their costumes on with ease, and made them look as if they were somehow glamorous and not itchy pieces of nonsense. And huddled in one corner, still in her normal clothes, was Rose.

Elsie slipped past me. "Your crazy girl is broken," she whispered loudly, tilting her head. I nearly kicked her, but she was too fast – she was already out of the hut before I could do it.

Glaring after her, I went over to the corner and crouched down. "Rose? Is something wrong?"

She started to shake her head, and then a moment later slowly nodded.

"You don't want to get changed? I don't blame you. These things are nasty." I tugged at the old, sagging wool. I imagined our Aunt Sara would wear something glamorous and flowery made of new nylon, and here we were dressed like sacks.

Rose shook her head again, and then finally she said: "Can't swim." There was fear in her eyes.

I took hold of her arm. "Don't worry about it. You can just sit in the boat. I'll tell Miss Bowler, shall I?"

She just bit her lip in response and stared at the floor. I decided to take that as a yes.

Scrambling back up again, I pushed past some of the other girls (causing a small chorus of "Watch where you're going!") and stepped out of the hut. It was warm outside, but I still didn't think it was warm enough to only be wearing a bathing suit. Miss Bowler was standing by the door as she waited for everyone to change.

"Miss," I tugged on her sleeve, "Rose can't swim. Can she just sit in the boat?"

"Pah! There's no such thing as *can't*!" Miss Bowler thundered.

I frowned at her. "I really don't think she can, Miss. She's scared to death. She could *drown*."

Miss Bowler must have noticed my emphasis, because some of the colour drained from her face. The school was trying to recover from the terrible reputation that our previous headteachers had given it, and another drowned student would really not look good in the newspapers.

"None of your cheek," she said. "Well, fine." She raised a warning finger. "But she'd better put some rowing in."

* * *

It wasn't long before we were back on the shore in our group – or mostly in our group, because Elsie was avoiding standing near us as much as possible.

"Right!" Miss Bowler blew her whistle, the shrill sound piercing into my ears. Rose jumped. "Choose your boat, one group at a time!"

I was in front, so I took charge and hopped up on to the jetty, the others following close behind me. The wet planks were covered in algae and they wobbled as I walked over them.

All the rowing boats were fairly similar, made of curved wood with a pair of oars in the middle. They all looked like they'd been sitting on that lake for years, through all weathers, just waiting for someone to find them. They had optimistic names painted on the side, though they were peeling and hard to read. I wanted to choose one that spoke to me. *Serenity. Hope. Skylark.* One that either said *Charity* or *Chastity*. One of them looked like it said *Cabbage*, and I couldn't quite figure out what that was meant to be.

But I went past all of these, and I picked the boat that was named *Adventure*.

Unfortunately the *Adventure* didn't quite look like it would live up to its name. There was a small crack in the hull and the benches were worn in the middle. It wobbled as I climbed into it, and the smell of damp wood hit my nose.

Ivy looked down at me from the jetty. "Are you sure about this?" she asked, her voice wobbling almost as much as the boat.

"Not one bit," I grinned.

With a sigh, Ivy climbed in beside me and sat down heavily on the bench at the back. Ariadne followed, with a few anxious glances around at where she'd left her precious camera on the shore. Then came Rose, still wearing all her clothes and hugging herself.

"It's all right," Ivy said, holding out a hand to her and helping her climb in. But Rose didn't seem at all reassured. She sat down and clung to the bench so tightly that her knuckles went white.

"Where's the harpy?" I asked, looking around. I wasn't at all surprised to see that Elsie was still gossiping on the shore.

"Sparks!" Miss Bowler barked. "Get in your group!"

"Sorry, Miss!" said Elsie, hurrying over. I half hoped she might slip on the jetty, but we had no such luck. She untied the boat from the post it was anchored to and then thudded into it, sending it rocking and splashing water over the sides.

"Watch it!" I snapped at her. Rose looked like she was going to be sick.

Elsie ignored me and simply sat in the front, lying back

and spreading her arms out. "What are you waiting for?" she said, with a smirk. "Start rowing."

I glared at her. "Who died and made you queen of the boat?"

"I'm the prefect; you do what I say." Elsie put her feet up on the middle bench, between me and Ivy. *Ugh.*

Ivy leant over and whispered: "Just pretend she isn't here."

Fine, I thought. *I can do that.*

I'd never rowed anything before, but I had a vague idea of how it worked. I grabbed hold of one of the oars, while Ivy took the other. We began pulling on them, pushing the water out of the way as the boat juddered into action.

In the distance, the surface of the lake was as grey as the sky. Close up, you could see the bottom – stones and weeds and flickers of tiny fish. I thought for a second about the village that lay down there somewhere, and wondered if you could swim to it. I imagined myself tumbling down through the buildings, lungs full of water, skeletal hands reaching up from below to pull me down...

"Scarlet," Ivy moaned. "We're going round in circles!"

"Sorry," I muttered, and started rowing properly again. I tried to ignore the smug expression on Elsie's face.

* * *

Our boats were soon out in the middle of the glassy lake, forming a circle as the wind ruffled our hair. The final boat was headed up by Miss Bowler. Ariadne was holding her fingers out to make a rectangle, framing the lake for imaginary photographs. Rose still hadn't looked up.

Miss Bowler cupped her hands to her mouth, as if she needed any help boosting her volume. "RIGHT! FIRST SWIMMERS IN!"

I gulped and looked at Ivy. Given who we were with, that was probably us. We stood up together, trying very hard not to rock the boat. Predictably, Elsie started trying to cause us as much difficulty as possible. She shuffled from side to side, making the boat sway awkwardly in the water.

"Will you stop that?" I demanded.

"Miss Bowler said to get in," said Elsie. "So you're going."

I'll show her, I thought. *I'll show everyone*. Taking a deep breath and squeezing my eyes shut, I leapt up in the air and plummeted into the icy water.

It hit me in a rush, then I kicked my legs until I bobbed up to the surface again, gasping in air. "Cold!" I yelled.

Ivy and I had learnt to swim in the brook near our house in hot summers, but this was different. The lake water was colder, for one, and we were much further from shore. But my body took over and soon I was swimming in loops round the boat.

Seeing that I hadn't drowned or been eaten by anything, others started to jump in too. I looked up to see Ivy standing in the boat, trying hard not to tip it over.

"Do it!" I shouted at her, treading water with a big grin on my face. "It's not so bad!"

She didn't look convinced, but seeing everyone else dropping over the sides of their boats seemed to encourage her. She held her nose and jumped into the water beside me with a huge splash.

I laughed, but I noticed the boat was still rocking and Rose was still huddled up nervously, with her collar hiding the chain of her necklace.

"Someone needs to stay in the boat to make sure it doesn't float away," said Ariadne as Ivy came to the surface, shivering.

"That'll be me, then," said Elsie. "Go on, you two."

"Rose can't swim," said Ariadne.

"Oh, really?" said Elsie. I didn't like the expression on her face one bit. She stood up, the boat swaying with her movements, and clambered over to where Rose sat. "Maybe it's time you tried," she said. And in one swift movement, she'd pushed Rose straight into the water.

Chapter Nineteen

Ivy

Rose screamed as she fell. The sound pierced my ears. Without even thinking, forgetting that I even had any fear, I dived after her.

I peeled my eyes open and saw her sinking, the sight strange and rippled by the water. Her mouth was open, still screaming wordlessly, and then she started kicking and thrashing about.

I knew I had only moments to reach her.

For a few horrible seconds, I thought I wasn't going to make it – that she was just going to keep tumbling into the lake forever. But I grabbed her, then suddenly realised that Scarlet was beside me, her hair flowing around her face. Together we took hold of Rose and kicked upwards as hard as we could.

We hefted Rose out of the water, and I felt her weight disappear from my arms. As we surfaced, drinking in the air, I heard her gasping and choking.

I pushed my wet hair out of my eyes, and blinked them dry, to see that there was now another boat beside us. Miss Bowler had dragged Rose up into it.

"Are you all right?" she was saying. "Speak up, girl!"

Rose didn't speak up at the best of times, and I couldn't imagine that she was going to when she had a mouthful of water. But her eyes were open, and she was breathing, although it was in stuttering gulps. She nodded slowly.

I bobbed in the water, trying to keep my muscles moving so that I wouldn't freeze.

Scarlet was doing the same, and she looked furious. "Miss! Elsie pushed her in!"

"I didn't," said Elsie indignantly.

"Yes, you did," Ariadne pointed out, "I was right in front of you!"

Miss Bowler turned, nearly tipping her boat over in the process. "Is this true, Sparks?"

"She slipped," Elsie said, spreading her arms out.

But our swimming teacher was not amused. "What are the three Ss of Swimming, Sparks?"

"There's only one S in swimming," she muttered.

"WRONG!" Miss Bowler barked. "They are Safety, Safety and Safety! Back to the shore you go!"

"But, Miss—" Elsie began to protest.

I swam nearer to the boat and held on to the side. Even on a lake, there were waves from the wind. "What about Ariadne, Miss?"

"Flitworth can get in the water and come back in our boat," the teacher ordered. "Off with you, Sparks!"

Ariadne stood up, looking completely uncertain.

"It's all right!" I called out to her. "Just a bit cold!"

"I'm not a good swimmer either," she called back. She rubbed her arms and stamped her feet. "All right," she said finally. "I'm coming in!"

I watched as Ariadne jumped up and plunged, completely ungracefully, into the lake. "Ack!" she cried as she came to the surface. "Reallyreally*really* cold!"

"I know," I said with a smile. I reached out and pulled her over to Miss Bowler's boat, so that she could hold on to it too.

We watched as Elsie furiously rowed away, a scowl twisting her features. "I hope your arms hurt!" Scarlet yelled after her.

Miss Bowler wrapped Rose in a towel. Rose's skin was whiter than white and her teeth were chattering.

"Did I drop it?" she whispered suddenly. "Did I drop it?" Her hand shot to her neck, and then she frantically patted at her jumper until she eventually found the golden chain of the locket. I heard her breathe a loud sigh of relief.

"Are you all right now, Rose?" I asked. Her nod was a lot faster this time.

Miss Bowler patted her on the back, making her cough up more lake water. "We'll keep her in the boat this time," Miss Bowler said.

After the awful incident was over, things started to brighten up. The day was getting warmer, and I slowly got used to the temperature of the water. Scarlet and I swam across the circle of boats, and tried to show Ariadne how to move her arms and legs in the right way. Father had taught us to swim in a rare moment of happiness in our childhood, before he married Edith. I remembered him laughing as Scarlet and I doggy-paddled across the brook; how he smiled and ruffled our hair. As the memory came to my mind, I felt a pang of something, and realised that – however strange it was – I actually missed our father.

We kept checking up on Rose, who seemed to be recovering well enough now that she was safe out of the water, though I could tell she wouldn't be happy until she was back on dry land.

We swam however we liked, practised diving, hung off the boats. It was so much better than being forced to do lengths of Rookwood's horrible pool, though I thought Miss Bowler would have preferred it if that had been what we were doing.

"Do you think we're near the village?" Scarlet asked me at one point.

"No idea!" I replied. All I could see when I dipped my head in the water was shreds of weeds and the odd silvery fish darting by. The bottom of the lake was deep, deep down.

Eventually I got tired, and clambered up into Miss Bowler's boat (with help). Scarlet followed. Ariadne seemed to have taken to swimming, however, and was still going, enthusiastically bobbing around.

But moments later, as we sat shivering in the bottom of the boat, she cried out.

I immediately leant over the side. "Ariadne!"

"What's wrong?" Scarlet asked her.

Ariadne was flailing her arms. "Something touched my foot!" She scrambled over to us. "Pull me out, pull me out!"

"Nonsense, Flitworth," said Miss Bowler. "Buck up."

"I'm serious!" Ariadne cried.

I believed her, and I knew Scarlet would too. We both

reached out and hauled her up, where she tipped awkwardly over the side and lay with her legs flapping like a recently caught fish. We pulled her back upright.

"What happened?" I asked. "What did it feel like?"

She shuddered, and I put my arm round her. "Like a hand grabbing at my foot," she said darkly.

The cold pricked at my skin. Whatever had touched Ariadne, something was not right about the lake. I found myself longing for the shore.

Miss Bowler rowed us back, and the boat sped across the water even though she was manning the oars alone. She was surprisingly muscular for someone who never seemed to actually swim herself. The other boats trailed after us.

Elsie was waiting beside the jetty, looking miserable, having haphazardly tied up the *Adventure*. And as we climbed out and wrapped ourselves in the threadbare towels, I noticed that she was holding Ariadne's camera.

"Hey!" I called out. "That's Ariadne's."

Elsie looked up. "I know," she said.

I looked around for Miss Bowler, hoping she would give Elsie a telling-off again, but she was already fussing with the other boats.

Ariadne ran down off the jetty. "Put it down, please! My daddy gave it to me!"

"*My daddy gave it to me,*" Elsie sneered back, mimicking her nastily.

I took a step forward, but Cassandra had already spotted her friend and was hopping down beside her, easily making the drop. "Give me a look, Else," she said. Ariadne watched in horror as one prefect threw the camera to the other. I could've sworn that time stood still for a moment.

"No," Ariadne whimpered. "Don't..."

Cassandra threw the camera back again, while Ariadne trailed between the two of them, hopelessly trying to catch it.

I watched as my twin darted down, running across the pebbles. She stood, fists clenched, in front of Cassandra, who towered over her. I knew there was nothing I could do to stop my sister adding fuel to the fire.

"What do you think you're doing?" she demanded. "Give that back to Ariadne, right now!"

Cassandra just laughed, and dangled the camera high above Scarlet's head. There was a flicker of anger on Scarlet's face, and then suddenly a sweet smile appeared. "Uh-oh," I whispered. I knew that smile. She was up to something.

Scarlet ran off to the hut where we'd got changed, without looking back.

"What is she playing at?" Elsie laughed. "Giving up already?"

And then Scarlet reappeared, carrying a pile of clothes. I realised what she was doing.

"Oi!" Cassandra yelled. "Are those ours? What the—"

She lowered the camera, and Ariadne grabbed it right out of her hand, but Scarlet had got the prefects' attention.

My twin now had a look of intense determination, but she made sure to grin at the prefects as she ran past them. And before they had time to react, she threw all of their clothes straight into the lake.

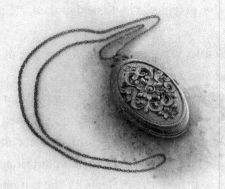

Chapter Twenty

SCARLET

M iss Bowler was furious, but it was absolutely worth it.

I got Ariadne's camera back safely, and the expressions on Elsie and Cassandra's faces were priceless. Even more priceless was seeing them frantically splashing around in the water as they tried to pick up their clothes.

Since there was no such thing as a detention on a school trip, I was instead banished back to the hotel to write a hundred lines of *I will not throw people's things in the lake*

(Miss Bowler had absolutely no imagination). I laughed to myself all the way back up the hill, remembering Elsie's mouth contorting in rage.

As I got closer to the Shady Pines, there was a loud rustling in the undergrowth beside me. I stopped in my tracks, suddenly realising that I was on my own. What if it was a ghost? Or a bear?

I decided that, whatever it was, my best bet was to shout at it. "Who's there?" I yelled.

And a moment later, I almost jumped out of my skin as Julian popped out of the bushes.

"Oh, hello!" His hair was sticking up at funny angles and there were leaves in it. "Sorry! Did I startle you?"

I tried to pretend I hadn't just been about to run screaming back to the hotel. "Not at all," I said.

He smiled and waved his binoculars at me. "Just hiding out in the hopes that I might spot something rare. Are you keeping an eye out for birds?"

I looked around. "Well, I can see three crows and..." I stared back down the hill. "A seagull, I think."

He laughed. "Good work. I'm off to the hide, now. Stay out of trouble. Enjoy yourself." He tipped an invisible hat at me, and then walked off into the woods.

"I'll enjoy writing lines!" I called after him.

* * *

As I reached the hotel, the chill of the lake wearing off and the heat seeping in, I realised that I didn't actually have anything to write lines *with*. With a sigh, I went up to the reception desk, where Mrs Rudge was sitting, staring into space.

"Hullo, Mrs Rudge," I said.

She looked up sharply. "Nothing's wrong!"

"I... didn't say it was?" What a weird lady. "I wondered if I could borrow some paper and a pencil?"

"Oh." Her eyes went down to the desk. "Of course." She fumbled around in a drawer and produced some for me. "Enjoy yourself," she added.

"Why does everyone keep saying that?" I muttered.

I ran into Mrs Knight in the hallway. "Scarlet?" she said. "What are you doing back here?"

"Have to write lines, Miss," I said.

She frowned at me. "Whatever did you do?"

I looked at my feet. "I may have thrown Elsie and Cassandra's clothes in the lake..."

When I looked back up at her, I could have sworn she was trying not to laugh. "Well, that was very bad behaviour. I expect better from you."

"Do you?" I asked. I genuinely wondered.

"Sometimes," she replied. "Right, into your room, then.

We'll see you at supper, and I want you to behave this time, please."

"Yes, Miss," I said. "Of course, Miss."

I made it back to our room, and I checked everything, staring into our suitcases and peering into the cupboards. It all seemed to be in order. Relieved, I set about writing lines.

A while later, the others came barrelling back in.

"That was brilliant!" Ariadne cried, dropping her camera on to the bed. She hugged me enthusiastically. Ivy and Rose were still grinning. "You showed them!"

I grinned back. "I did. Though I think Miss Bowler showed me in return. I'm sick of writing these." I threw the piece of paper on to the carpet.

"Elsie and Cassandra had to walk back to the hotel in their swimsuits," Ivy said. Her smile faded. "It was *rather* funny, but I think they'll be out to get us even more now."

"Ha," I said. "They can try."

Ariadne pulled out her suitcase full of photography supplies. "Thank you so much for saving my camera, Scarlet. I'm going to go down and ask if they have a darkroom here, or just a... well, a room that's dark."

"Why?" I asked.

She pointed at the camera. "The roll of film is full. I need

177

to change it, and you have to do that in the dark, or all of the film gets exposed."

I blinked at her. I hadn't the faintest idea how a camera worked. She didn't seem to notice.

"It would be wonderful if I could develop them," she continued. "Then I can see if I've got any good ones."

"I'm sure they're lovely," said Ivy pleasantly.

I rolled my eyes as Ariadne picked up all her equipment and headed out of the room. "At least she didn't make me pose for them this time..."

At dinner, we had vegetable soup and fresh bread with cold cuts of meat. I gulped it down, starving after all the swimming.

Ariadne arrived with a spring in her step. "Well, would you believe it? Mr Rudge has a darkroom."

"Really?" Ivy asked. "He likes photography, then?"

"It's down in the basement. He said they have a lot of guests who come to photograph the scenery, and he decided to take it up as a hobby. I think it was the least grumpy thing I've ever heard him say." Ariadne giggled. "All his photographs just seemed to be of trees, though."

"So where are the ones you took? I'm surprised you haven't put on an exhibition already," I teased.

"You have to leave them to dry," she replied, as if that was obvious. "I'll go down and get them later."

I got up and handed my lines to Miss Bowler, who glared at them and said she hoped I'd learnt my lesson. I said I certainly wouldn't throw anyone's things in a lake ever again, and I felt fairly sure that I wasn't lying. There was no sign of the harpies, which was amusing. I hoped they'd stay away from us now. I imagined them sitting in their room, silently fuming.

When I returned to our table, the conversation had turned back to the day's events. "I'm telling you, something touched my leg," Ariadne said. "It was incredibly scary." Though I had to say, she sounded more excited than scared.

"There is something going on with the lake, I swear it," Ivy said. "And this hotel. But nothing adds up."

"Maybe *we're* the ones who are haunted," I said through a mouthful of bread. "Strange things seem to happen to us everywhere we go." I thought for a moment about our mother, about how her shadow had appeared in my dreams. I'd hoped she was watching over us.

My thoughts were interrupted by Cassandra bowling through the restaurant, nearly knocking over the lady in the wheelchair. She came to a halt beside our table and dropped a necklace right into the middle of it.

"What is this?" she demanded.

I looked at it. "Looks like a necklace to me. A gold one. With a locket."

Cassie leant over the table. "It's *my* necklace," she fumed. "And we just found it in *your* room."

I clenched my fists. "What were you doing going through our things?"

"Well, you had no problem throwing our things in the lake. I knew you little brats were up to something," she snarled. "So we decided to do a search. And we found this in *her* bed." She pointed at Rose, whose eyes went wide. "So she is a thief, AND a freak."

Everyone was staring. Mrs Knight had noticed the commotion, and she rushed over. "What's going on, girls?"

Cassandra straightened up again and smiled sweetly. "Nothing, Miss. I just found my necklace, is all. I was just letting everyone know."

"Oh, well, that is good news," said Mrs Knight. "Carry on, then." She wandered back to where she had been standing and supervising, looking envious of the food on plates as she went past.

Cassandra leant back down, and stared intently at Rose. "I know what you are," she said.

Rose jumped up, her soup spilling on the white tablecloth. With one last look at Cassandra, she ran out of the room.

"A dirty thief!" Cassandra finished, fists clenched, and then she too stormed away.

* * *

180

"What just happened?" Ivy asked, baffled.

I shook my head. "I have no idea. But..." I played through the afternoon in my mind. "I looked through our room when I got back, to see if anyone had taken anything. And it didn't look like anything had been touched or moved. Do you think Cassandra just planted the necklace?"

"I wouldn't be surprised." Ariadne sighed.

One of the maids hurried over and began cleaning up the soup, so we paused for a moment. We thanked her, and she gave us a distracted smile.

"Either that," said Ivy, looking worried as the maid bustled away, "or Rose actually took it." She paused. "But she wouldn't do that. Would she?"

"Of course not," said Ariadne. "*Of course not.*" She didn't look entirely convinced. "I'm sure I would have noticed if there were a necklace in our bed."

"Unless it was hidden in a pillow or something," Ivy pointed out.

"Or in the mattress," I suggested.

"And..." Ivy leant forward and lowered her voice. "Why did Rose react like that, when Cassandra said she knew what she was?"

We all looked at each other. None of us wanted to say it, but... maybe there was something going on with Rose. Could we really trust her?

Chapter Twenty-one

Ivy

We found Rose huddled in a corner of the hotel room. She had a blanket pulled tightly round her. We tried to ask her if she was all right, but her silence had returned. This time, she didn't even mime an answer. She simply stared at the wall. It was at times like this that I missed Violet, who had always seemed to be able to communicate with her.

I was going to avoid asking about the necklace, because I didn't want to upset her any further. Scarlet, however, was not so tactful. "You didn't take her locket, did you?" she asked. There was no response.

"We should give her some space," I said. Cassandra's comment had clearly distressed Rose. I knelt down beside her. She was softly shaking beneath the blanket. "I'm sorry about all this," I said. "Do you want us to go away for a bit?"

Her eyes flicked over to me, and she nodded very slowly.

That decided it. I herded the others back out of the room.

"Just one problem with this," said Scarlet.

"Um, yes," said Ariadne. "We're supposed to be going to bed. Where are we going to go?"

"We could go and steal some more soup?" Scarlet suggested. I didn't even bother dignifying that with an answer.

I looked up and down the corridor. Some of the doors were open, with a few of the girls heading out to use the lavatory or brush their teeth. There were some separate bathrooms as well, which was a relief, because I hadn't fancied using the bath in the middle of the room in the first place, let alone after the strange incident where it had filled up by itself. The familiar smell of the oil lamps swam on the air.

Nadia popped out of the door to the room she was

sharing with Anna, carrying a towel and a toothbrush. "Oh!" she exclaimed as she nearly ran into us. "What was all that about at dinner? Are they still angry about their clothes getting soaked? Because personally, I found that rather hilarious."

"Cassandra thinks Rose stole her necklace. We think Cassandra is an enormous idiot." That was Scarlet's contribution. She was staring at the paintings that lined the corridor.

"Sounds fair enough to me. Those prefects think they're so much better than everyone else. And they definitely have it in for you now." Nadia sighed. "I wish Penny was here."

That was something I had never thought I'd hear anyone say, but there was no accounting for taste, I supposed. Penny seemed to have calmed down a little after the ballet, and I hoped she might have improved for good.

"Not enjoying being Penny-less?" Scarlet jibed.

"Never been penniless in my life," Nadia shot back with a wink. "But Penny is my friend. And she wouldn't let those two be top dog. Anyway," she said. "You ought to watch your backs. And watch Rose's back, especially, where they're concerned." With a quick nod, she darted away towards the bathrooms.

Ariadne's brow wrinkled. "Do you really think something's going to happen?"

"I doubt it," said Scarlet. "And we don't need Penny. They won't get past me."

In the end we sneaked downstairs and went on to the veranda that ran across the front of the hotel, looking out over the lake, to watch the sunset. Ariadne leant over the balcony to take photographs. The lady in the wheelchair was out there too, a blanket draped over her legs, and Phyllis and Julian were chatting at a table in the corner. I wanted to ask Phyllis where she'd got to the day before, but she was deep in conversation and I couldn't work up the courage. She'd probably just gone hiking.

When the sun was finally down, the pinks and oranges melting into black clouds and a sprinkle of stars dusting the sky, we began to shiver. Even though it could be hot during the day, the nights were still chilly.

At that point, Miss Bowler marched out and ordered us to get to bed, and we didn't want to argue – though Ariadne took the chance to run down to the darkroom and collect her pictures.

Back in the room, Rose had gone to bed. She seemed to be sleeping peacefully, and I felt relieved. But even then, I wondered about the necklace. What if Rose really had taken it? I didn't think she would do it for selfish reasons, but what if she'd done it by accident, or for some other reason that we hadn't considered? I wanted to ask her, but it was horrible seeing her so upset. Her past, what she'd said about her family and what they did to her... was that tied up in this somewhere?

I was so tired that my eyes were slowly slipping shut. I pulled on my nightgown, climbed into the enormous bed beside my twin, and fell fast asleep.

There was a noise.

I sat upright. I had been sleeping soundly, and now I was awake. What had happened?

I blinked in the darkness. The strange room swam in front of my eyes, nothing but blurred shapes.

There's no moon, I thought. *It's too dark to see.*

I reached for one of Ariadne's many candles, standing in a holder next to the bed. There was a matchbook beside it. I fumbled, then managed to strike a match. As I put it to the wick, the candle flickered into action.

I held it out, looking around the room. Scarlet was stirring beside me, but hadn't quite woken. I slipped my legs out of the bed and tiptoed over to the far wall, the draught from the fireplace swirling in cold tendrils around my legs. As I peered at the other bed, I realised that Rose was missing.

A thousand thoughts ran through my head. Was she

upset again? Had she just gone to the lavatories? Or was it something more sinister?

Whatever it was, I knew I wouldn't be able to get back to sleep unless I found out. Rose might need help. I tiptoed towards the door of the room, peeled it open gently and crept out into the corridor.

I looked left and right, bathing the walls in the glow of the candle, and decided to go left first. Closed doors passed me on both sides, none of them betraying what might lie behind them. I presumed Rose wouldn't be found in anyone else's room, especially not the one where the teachers slept.

I decided to try the bathrooms and lavatories next. I peered into each one, but all the doors were unlocked, and there was no sign of Rose.

Or so I thought. Until I looked down at the corridor carpet.

There were wet footprints, roughly the size of Rose's feet, forming a trail from one of the bathrooms towards another door.

Cautiously, I went over and tried the handle. The room was unlocked. I took a deep breath, and opened the door.

It was a room not dissimilar to ours, but with only one large bed and some sofas. The bed was made, and the whole room looked untouched. I supposed it hadn't been rented out. But it also featured a pair of glass-panelled doors. They were flung wide open, leading outside.

And there, in the middle of the balcony, stood Rose.

I stepped closer quietly, not wanting to startle her, and noticed something was off. Her hair was soaking wet, and so were her clothes. In fact, why was she even wearing her day clothes and not a nightgown? Another step, and I could see that her dress was buttoned up wrongly, and her jumper was on back to front.

"Rose?" I whispered softly.

She didn't seem to hear me. Another step. Her eyes were open and glassy, staring at nothing. I couldn't breathe. Something was very wrong.

Another step, and now I was through the glass doors and out in the cold night air. "Rose?" I tried again. "Rose?" I reached out and touched her sleeve.

And she screamed.

I jumped backwards, hand on my heart, and nearly dropped the candle holder.

Rose blinked, too many times, and then suddenly the glassy look was gone from her eyes and she seemed to see me.

"Ivy?" she said in a voice barely above a whisper. She looked around fearfully.

I could finally breathe again. "Are you all right? Rose, you're all wet! And you're standing out on a balcony in the middle of the night!"

She felt frantically for the necklace at her throat, then wrapped her arms round herself and started shivering, her teeth chattering.

"Come inside," I said. I led her into the room and pulled the doors shut. "Do you know what happened?"

She shook her head. Her pale cheeks began to burn red.

It began to dawn on me what might be going on. I'd said it myself, hadn't I? *What if she sleepwalks?*

"Rose," I tried gently. "Do you... walk in your sleep?"

There were a few moments of silence. "Sometimes."

I felt a sliver of relief growing in my mind. That's what was going on. "I think that's what's happened. You got dressed in your sleep –" I gestured at her buttons and jumper – "and tried to get in the bathtub. That must be why your clothes are wet."

She frowned. "Bad," she said simply.

That threw me a little. "Bad? To sleepwalk?"

This time it was a nod.

"But it's not your fault," I said. I put my hand on her damp sleeve again. "You can't help it if you're asleep. I sleepwalked once in my Aunt Phoebe's house, and I woke up lying on the kitchen floor!"

She bent over, her wet hair dripping on to the carpet. "They said…" She didn't seem to want to finish the sentence. I wondered who she meant. Had her family said it was bad? The doctors in the asylum?

And a part of me wondered if she meant she did something bad while sleepwalking. *Stealing?*

"Scared," she said, still shaking. I wrapped an arm round her.

"It's all right. Don't be frightened." I tried not to think about the sight of her standing on the balcony. I had been frightened out of my wits. "Come on. Let's go back to our room so you can get dry."

Eventually, she inhaled deeply and then responded with another nod.

I helped her to her feet and we headed for the door, Rose still dripping. I prayed that the water would dry before the next morning. I didn't want the Rudges to have a heart attack.

But as we stepped out into the corridor, things went even more wrong.

Because Elsie and Cassandra were standing there, holding candles of their own, and they looked *furious*.

"There she is!" Elsie cried. "*Get her!*"

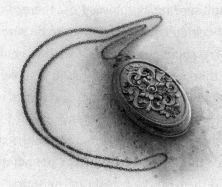

Chapter Twenty-two

SCARLET

I was woken by the sound of raised voices and footsteps out in the corridor. I was sure there had been a candle beside our bed, but when I felt for it in the dark, it seemed to have gone.

Something else was gone too. *Ivy.*

I blinked in the darkness. The shouting grew louder and then faded. As if someone were being chased.

My twin senses were telling me something was wrong. I jumped out of bed and felt my way towards the door. I could hear Ariadne still snoring, but... was Rose there? I couldn't hear her, and I couldn't see well enough to be sure.

I didn't worry about being quiet. Ariadne could sleep through most things, and Ivy might be in trouble. Maybe Rose too. I dashed out into the corridor and turned my head quickly from side to side. Where had they gone? I thought I could hear echoes of shouting coming from the stairway.

I ran towards the sound, my footsteps pounding on the floor. I followed them all the way down the stairs, running blindly along the hallway until I came to the reception area. The lights were still lit there, but the Rudges must have long since gone to bed. The front door of the hotel was just swinging shut as I reached it.

"Oh no, you don't," I said, grabbing it before it could close. I ran out into the night.

The courtyard in front of the hotel was lit up, and misty rain was falling.

I saw Ivy and Rose backed up against a wall, and two taller shapes that were unmistakably Elsie and Cassandra. I cursed them under my breath.

"No escape now, freak," I heard Cassandra say.

I crept nearer, the rain sticking my hair to my face. If the harpies couldn't see me, I had an advantage.

"Leave her alone," Ivy said. She was holding a candle that spluttered in the wind. "She's never done anything to you."

The air was cold. I tried to forget that I was only wearing a nightgown and a pair of stockings. I tiptoed, staying light on my feet.

"We know it was you!" Elsie was shrieking. "We practically caught you red-handed!"

"We have no idea what you're talking about," Ivy pleaded. Her eyes flickered over to me, and I knew that she had seen me. I put my finger to my lips. She quickly looked away again.

As I got closer, I could see that Rose was soaking wet. *The rain?* I thought for a moment, but no, she looked like she'd fallen in the lake again. What on earth had just happened?

Cassandra was shaking with anger. "You stole my necklace," she said. "And then you break into our room while we're sleeping! How dare you? How DARE YOU?" She reached out as if she were going to slap Rose...

And I caught her arm in mid-swing.

She spun round furiously. "What—"

"You are *not* going to touch her," I said.

She may have been taller than me, but she wasn't stronger. I kept my grip on her arm as she tried to wrestle it away from me.

"Rose, run!" I yelled.

She didn't need to be told twice. Rose was small and

quick, and she darted round Cassandra and back off towards the hotel.

"Elsie!" Cassandra tried to alert her friend, but Ivy reacted faster than Elsie could. She stuck out her leg and sent Elsie flying. I almost cheered.

"Either of you want to explain what this is about?" I demanded.

Elsie got up and brushed herself off, her face red. I thought she was about to start steaming. "Don't have to explain ourselves to you," she muttered.

"Maybe not," I said. "But I can go and tell Mrs Knight that you two just attacked my sister and my friend for no good reason. Or –" I tugged Cassandra's arm a little to make the point – "you could tell us what you've got your knickers in a twist about."

"She knows," Elsie said with a glare at Ivy as she scrambled back up to her feet.

"I really don't," said Ivy.

Cassandra shared a glance with Elsie – I think they realised Ivy was telling the truth. "If you let me go, I'll tell you."

I shared a glance with my twin. I didn't really trust Cassandra, but it was worth a try.

I dropped her arm and watched as she rubbed it, trying to get the feeling back.

"I'm not going to wait out here all night," I said. Not least because it was so cold and rainy. "I'm running straight for the teachers if you don't explain."

"All right, all right." Cassandra glared at me. She patted down her usually perfect curls, which were going frizzy in the rain. "We heard noises in our room," she finally explained. "And when we lit the lights, we saw our room had been... *vandalised*."

That reminded me of what had happened to us. Ivy must have thought the same, because she asked: "Things thrown everywhere? Curtains ripped?"

"No, not like that. There was this message written on the wall. In red. Like blood." Cassandra shuddered. Elsie looked sick. "And there was water all over the floor. Then we came out into the corridor and saw that *freak*, soaking wet."

"It was *her*," Elsie hissed into the misty air. "You're all blind. You think she's so sweet and quiet. She's *insane*, Grey. Haven't you heard? She was in a mental asylum!"

"So was I," I said through gritted teeth, but I don't think they heard me. Elsie was in full flow now.

"She's crazy. She hardly talks. She's a thief. And now this? Soaking wet and writing threats on our wall? She should never have come on this trip. It's not safe for any of us." Elsie started punching one hand into the other. "She. Is. Crazy!"

Ivy wiped rain out of her eyes. "What exactly did this threat say?"

Elsie and Cassandra glanced at each other.

Ivy's candle gave one final splutter and went out.

"Maybe you should see for yourself," Elsie said quietly.

The prefects marched back into the Shady Pines Hotel, and we followed behind them.

"Are you all right?" I whispered to Ivy.

"Fine," she replied. "Just cold. I hope Rose is safe in our room now. She was sleepwalking."

I nodded my agreement as understanding dawned. So Rose had sleepwalked out of our room?

Ivy found some more matches behind the reception desk, and we relit the candle. As we slowly climbed the stairs to the top floor, I noticed that there were still wet footprints leading out of the bathroom.

"She got in the bath?" I asked Ivy.

"Seems so." Ivy shrugged.

I peered closer, and I realised that there were more footprints, heading towards the prefects' room. Ivy saw them too.

"That's not good," she said.

"Are you coming or not?" Elsie whispered angrily from over by their door.

"Yes, yes," I said, hurrying along. "Keep your hair on." But from a quick glance at the footprints, I could have sworn that they were bigger than Rose's.

Elsie held the door open, gesturing towards the wall with her other arm. Ivy and I stepped inside, and looked up.

I saw, in large, hastily painted letters as red as blood...

WE DO NOT SLEEP.
WE ARE WATCHING YOU.

Chapter Twenty-three

IVY

The terrifying writing was huge, angrily slashed across the wall.

"Now do you believe us?" Cassandra said.

I didn't know what to think. Rose had sleepwalked, and she'd got into the bath fully dressed. What was to say she hadn't painted this strange message? Those footprints...

"I really don't know," I said. I stepped back from the wall. I wanted to get as far away from the words as possible.

It didn't matter who had written them. They made the hairs on the back of my neck stand up.

Scarlet yawned. "I don't know either. You don't have proof it was her. And let's say it *was*—"

"It was!" Elsie snapped.

My twin ignored her. "Let's say it was. She was sleepwalking. She didn't do it on purpose."

"Firstly," said Cassandra, who was leaning against the bedpost with her arms folded, "that's if you believe her about the sleepwalking, and secondly, if she did it in her sleep, that's even *more* weird."

Elsie pointed out of the open door. "She's possessed. That's what it is."

I swallowed. I remembered Rose standing on the balcony, her eyes like glass. She had almost looked possessed.

"Well, if she's possessed, then blame the evil spirit that you think did it and not her," Scarlet said, rolling her eyes. She turned to leave. "I'm tired of this nonsense. It's the middle of the night."

"You expect us to go back to sleep with *this*?" Cassandra waved at the writing.

"You're supposed to be prefects. Why don't you go and tell the teachers?" I suggested. "Instead of attacking Rose?"

"*That would be too obvious*," Scarlet said in a stage whisper.

Both of them glared at us intently, and I decided it would definitely be a good time to leave. I took Scarlet's arm and led her out of the room before she decided to try to hit them.

"They probably painted it themselves," Scarlet muttered as the door slammed shut, leaving us with only the light of the little candle.

I tried to rub some of the warmth back into my body. Everything just felt too cold. "You don't think there's a chance that Rose... did this? You didn't see her when she was sleepwalking. It was really strange." I wasn't sure that even quite did justice to it. It was otherworldly, almost. "And you saw the footprints."

"I did," she said, her hand resting on the door handle to our room. "And I know it looks bad. But there's something off about them. They looked too big."

I scrunched up my face. "So someone else came in? But..." A memory came back to me. "The front door was bolted. I pulled it back when I ran in. They must lock up at night."

"So it was either someone staying at the hotel..." Scarlet mumbled.

"...or it was Rose," I finished. My brow furrowed. This wasn't right. I shouldn't think that way about her. She was just a frightened girl.

"Or," said Scarlet, "it was a ghost."

"It isn't a ghost," I insisted. But no matter how much I tried to keep it out, Mr Owens's story kept floating into my head. Those poor people, losing everything, even their graves...

We went back into the room, to find that Rose had fallen fast asleep in a chair in the corner, still wearing her wet clothes. There wasn't much we could do about it, so we draped the blanket over her and left her to sleep.

I blew the candle out and lay back in bed. Soon my eyelids were fluttering shut, and I dreamt of restless souls floating through the water. And, just on the edge of hearing, I could have sworn that I heard the echo of ringing bells...

The sun rose on another day at the Shady Pines. But it rose even more reluctantly than I did, and hid behind the clouds as soon as it got the chance.

I stared out at the lake as I brushed my hair. There were so many secrets beneath its surface, I was sure.

I'd wanted to talk to Rose, although I couldn't think what to say. "Did you really paint a creepy message on someone's wall while you were sleepwalking?" wouldn't be an easy question to ask or to answer.

Besides, Miss Bowler had already come to take Rose for questioning, so I hadn't had the chance. That meant that Elsie and Cassandra hadn't given up on accusing her, but at least they'd stopped taking matters into their own hands. I had tried to protest that Rose was innocent, and to explain about the sleepwalking, but Miss Bowler was too busy ranting to listen to me – no surprise there, I suppose.

We ate a distracted breakfast and tried to explain to Ariadne what had happened. The first thing she said was, "Do you think they'd let me photograph it?"

"I very much doubt it." I'd already seen Mr Rudge heading to the room with a bucket of whitewash and paintbrush. His face had been whiter than the contents of the bucket.

"You should have woken me up," she said, sounding disappointed.

"You were out like a light," Scarlet said. "And besides, it wasn't exactly a pleasant experience."

"Indeed," I added. "I'm crossing 'getting chased through the rain in my nightgown by angry prefects' off my list of things to ever do again."

"Fair enough," Ariadne said, but she didn't lift her eyes from her toast. "I hope Rose is all right."

We carried on eating in silence. Even with the other girls and guests there, the talk in the restaurant seemed so quiet compared to the usual racket of Rookwood's dining hall. I looked around at the different faces at each table, remembering what we'd said the night before – that either the message was supernatural, or the culprit was someone at the hotel.

The man with the green suit was sitting a few tables over, reading a newspaper. He hadn't given up on the hotel, then. Did he look tired, or guilty? It was hard to tell, especially when his face was partially obscured by his reading material. There was the lady in the wheelchair, though I imagined she probably wouldn't be able to get up to the top floor, let alone go about painting spooky messages and dripping water all over the carpet.

Besides that, there were some younger ladies who looked dressed for a hiking trip, all fresh-faced and giggly. There was a very elderly couple, both wearing outlandish hats. There were the Mosses, who were lovingly sharing a boiled egg on the next table over. And finally there was a man with a monocle and a moustache like a walrus, who was wearing a napkin like a bib.

I stared at every single one of them over breakfast, and learnt nothing. None of them seemed particularly the sort to be haunting a hotel, but then what was the sort? And why would they? What would be in it for them?

"It's useless," I said, keeping my voice low, and sighed. "I don't see how we can prove that Rose didn't do this, especially when I'm not even certain myself. But it couldn't be *real ghosts*... could it?"

"It would fit with the story," Ariadne said. "Maybe the spirits really are angry about what happened to the village. Maybe they're trapped under the water and can't get to heaven. Just think about it." She shuddered. "Not that I believe in ghosts, of course."

"Of course," Scarlet and I chorused.

"But wouldn't their souls go to heaven as soon as they died?" Scarlet asked. "Or do they wait around until their business is finished on earth?"

I shrugged. "I have no idea. I think we'll have to assume that a flesh-and-blood person is behind this. That leaves us with Rose. Or someone else at the hotel." I glanced around again furtively, but no one had seemed any more suspicious than when I'd first looked.

"I still think the harpies are doing it to themselves," Scarlet said. "It's just the sort of thing they'd do. They want to pin the blame on Rose. They've been terrible drags ever since she wouldn't show them her locket. I thought they were going to snap it off her neck."

"Even before that," Ariadne pointed out. "They wanted their friend to come on the trip, didn't they?"

I took a sip of my tea, trying to savour it. I would miss all this when we were back at Rookwood – the food, that is, not the haunted hotel. "But... they really did look genuinely scared about the writing. I suppose they could have messed up the rooms and planted Cassandra's necklace. But what about the bathtub filling up with water? And all the other things? The prayer book and the candlestick and the cross?"

"And if those things really are from the church under the lake..." Ariadne said, her eyes wide, "... if Elsie is responsible, or one of the other guests, or even Rose... how on earth would they have got them?"

"Could be fake," Scarlet said.

"But *why?* Why do any of that?" I really couldn't fathom it.

"I think someone wants us to be afraid," Scarlet replied darkly.

Suddenly I didn't feel like eating another bite of the breakfast. I *was* afraid.

Afraid she was right.

Chapter Twenty-four

SCARLET

I swore to myself that if the harpies were behind this, I was going to get them back, somehow. Whatever it took.

We returned to our room to find Rose crying. I didn't know what Miss Bowler had said to her, but we at least gathered that she hadn't been sent home or punished. I guessed Miss Bowler couldn't prove that Rose was guilty any more than we could.

Honestly, if she did want to scare the prefects, I didn't blame her. I couldn't imagine it, though. She had always seemed so sweet and friendly, even without using any words.

An image of her clutching the pony book that I'd given her came to mind. If Elsie and Cassandra opened their eyes for five minutes, maybe they could see her that way too.

But when we went back out into the corridor, hoping to find out what the day's activity was, we found Elsie protesting to Miss Bowler.

"But, *Miss*," she was saying. "We know she did it. We saw her. She was all wet and crazy-looking. She's mad, or she's possessed, or both!"

"How dare—" I started, but Ivy and Ariadne grabbed my arms and pulled me back into the doorway.

"This is all claptrap and twaddle!" said Miss Bowler. "I've never heard such balderdash in all my life! There's no such thing as being possessed. Someone vandalised your room, that's all. We'll get to the bottom of it." She shook her head.

Elsie decided to try a different approach. "But we saw her, right after. And she was all wet. She should be punished, shouldn't she? For vandalising? Or what's to stop her doing something worse?"

This time I wasn't going to let myself be held back. "Oh, you little snitch! You don't have proof that Rose has done anything!"

Elsie swung round. "Well, who do you think did it, then?"

I didn't have an answer for that. I just floundered uselessly.

207

"CALM DOWN, BOTH OF YOU!" Miss Bowler boomed. "Get back in your rooms and get ready for the day! We're going horse riding. I don't want to hear another word about this incident! Is that clear?"

"Yes, Miss," we all mumbled.

"I SAID, IS THAT CLEAR?"

"Yes, Miss!"

We made a hasty retreat back into the room.

"Did she..." Ivy paused. "Did she say *horse riding*?"

Ivy and I had only been on horseback a couple of times, when we were much younger. It had been at a farm near where we grew up. And they weren't horses at all, really, but tiny Shetland ponies. Father rode a big old mare called Chestnut, who was bad-tempered and would snort and flick her ears at you. She had these enormous chomping teeth and trying to feed her a carrot was a dangerous business.

Each time we'd gone riding I had hated it. I screamed the whole time and insisted I was going to fall off and die. Ivy had clung on for dear life, her face pale and eyes wide, not saying a word.

I wasn't hugely enthusiastic about the idea. "It's a horse," I kept saying. "They're big and angry. I don't think they want me to sit on them."

Ariadne, on the other hand, was overjoyed. "Oh, goody!"

she kept saying, clapping her hands. "Ever since Daddy sold Oswald I haven't been able to go riding. This will be such fun!"

It had cheered Rose up as well. At the mere mention of the word 'horse' she had dried her tears and was looking a lot more eager. "I'll help," she whispered, and suddenly she had pulled her boots on and dashed off out of the door.

"Help with what?" Ivy said after her.

"Preparing the horses for the ride, I suppose," Ariadne said. "Fetching their tack and grooming them and so on. I think she does that a lot at school."

I peered down at my suitcase and realised another problem – we didn't own any trousers. I definitely didn't fancy riding side-saddle. "Oh, look," I said. "We don't have any trousers. So we probably can't go anyway. Such a shame."

"You can both borrow some of mine!" Ariadne said cheerily.

I gave up and flopped on to the bed. It looked like I wasn't getting out of this one.

We went down to the courtyard once we were dressed, me trudging reluctantly and Ivy doing her best to look like she wasn't doing the same.

Ariadne was bouncier than ever, bounding down the

stairs with her camera round her neck as usual. She'd even found her own riding hat in one of her suitcases – goodness knows how it had fitted in there. Ivy had read a book called *Mary Poppins* about a nanny who had a magical bag that somehow managed to contain things like an armchair and a bedstead, and she was convinced Ariadne had one the same.

The weather was warm, but there were some angry black thunderclouds looming overhead, threatening to rain. The unsettled air smelt of pine and moss, with a strong undercurrent of horse.

Mrs Knight was standing in one corner of the courtyard, beckoning us all over. The drive continued round the corner there, to a large block of stables. I could hear some of the horses stomping and snorting already, and it reminded me of angry old Chestnut. I fought the urge to run back to our room and hide.

Mrs Rudge was standing in the stable yard – I guessed she owned the horses – along with a small group of local girls who were hurrying around. *They must help out here*, I thought. I spotted Rose carrying a saddle, and smiled. At least she was feeling better. I took the chance to glare at Elsie and Cassandra, who were muttering things to each other again. I wished they would get sent home.

I left Ivy chatting to Anna and wandered over to one of

the stalls. According to the door, the horse was called Daffodil. She looked at me warily and then went back to chewing hay.

Just then, Phyllis Moss popped up beside me. "Hello!" she said brightly. "Off for a ride, are we?"

"Apparently," I mumbled.

She didn't seem to notice my reluctance, looking at the horse instead. "Fine beast, isn't she? I was hoping I might be able to go for a ride myself." She turned to gaze around the stable yard.

"I don't think there'll be any horses left with all of us having a go," I pointed out.

She frowned. "You're probably right. Ah well, another day, then! Don't forget your orienteering skills if you get lost," she said with a wink.

"Is everyone here?" I heard Mrs Knight call out from the other side of the yard. She was standing on a mounting block and taking a quick head count, so I hurried back over.

"I'm here!" I announced to no one in particular. Ivy laughed at me.

"Right," said Mrs Knight. "Good morning, everyone! I know we've had some further trouble in the night, but let's put it all behind us, shall we?"

This time it was the prefects who glared at me. I pulled a face at them.

"Mrs Rudge runs these riding stables, and today we'll be having a go." Mrs Rudge curtsied, but I couldn't help noticing how preoccupied she looked. In fact, I could've sworn she'd flinched when Mrs Knight mentioned the events of last night.

Mrs Knight gestured to another lady who was already sitting astride a horse. "Mrs Hunt will be instructing us today and leading us on a hack."

"Good morning," Mrs Hunt said. She had a long, thin face, with blonde hair and an expression that seemed to indicate that no one was living up to her standards. She reminded me a lot of Miss Linton, who taught horse riding back at Rookwood. Just like Miss Linton, she wore a riding hat with a long coat and jodhpurs, her feet perfectly pointed in the stirrups. She was definitely dressed for the occasion – unlike Ivy and me, in our trousers that didn't fit properly.

Mrs Knight smiled. Miss Bowler, I noticed, was standing at the back of the courtyard, looking as if she had no intention of getting on a horse. I didn't blame her. I wondered if anyone would notice if I sidled over there...

"Get back here, Scarlet," the headmistress warned. Reluctantly I slunk back to my place in the crowd. "All right," she continued. "I'm sure you all know the basics of riding."

"Yes, Miss," most people chorused.

"Not really," I added.

Ivy gave me a look, and I could tell she was nervous. I hoped we'd both just remember how to do it.

"The girls have been helping to get everything ready," Mrs Knight said, gesturing at the stable girls and Rose, who was smiling shyly. "They're going to line the horses up and pick the best one for you to ride, based on your height. Then we're going to go on a fun adventure!"

I doubted it would be either fun or an adventure. But I had to grit my teeth and get on with it. I just hoped nothing would go horribly wrong this time.

Chapter Twenty-five

IVY

"Let's get started, then," Mrs Knight said. She clapped her hands, and Rose and the girls began to fetch each of the horses over. They looked so *tall*.

"I don't like the look of that one," Scarlet whispered, pointing to a huge black horse that reminded me uncomfortably of Raven, Miss Fox's horse. It was stamping angrily as Rose led it across the yard, its hooves clicking on the cobbles. Rose seemed unfazed, but I supposed she was used to that sort of thing.

I had to admit that I felt a little relieved when she led the horse to Mrs Knight instead of us.

Miss Bowler bustled around, putting us into height order. She spent a good amount of time trying to decide which way round to put me and Scarlet, even though I was fairly sure we were exactly the same height. She was a mirror image of me, after all. Scarlet was somewhat miffed when it was decided that I was taller. "Hmmph!" she declared loudly.

I hoped we might get some nice riding helmets, but no such luck – we were stuck with the awful ones that Miss Bowler had brought for caving. I at least got one that wasn't cracked this time, but it was rather worryingly wobbly instead.

The stable girls began helping people on to horses. Some were obviously more experienced and just jumped up with one foot in the stirrup. Others got a boost or used the mounting block. I had a suspicion that we'd need it too.

Eventually Rose came over and tugged at our sleeves. She seemed to be considerably happier – she was in her element, I supposed. She led us to a pair of almost identical grey horses – same height, same dappled coats, same saddles. She held her arms out, smirking as if she'd done something really funny.

"What?" Scarlet said suspiciously.

"Oh!" I exclaimed. "I get it! Grey twins! Like us!"

Rose laughed, nodding. Both of us grinned. I felt a pang of shame that I'd doubted her.

Another girl, short and wearing boyish dungarees, came over to help us get on. She told us that the horses were called Shadow and Whisper. Sweet names, but I still wasn't sure I wanted to ride either of them. They at least seemed calmer than some of the other horses I'd seen, standing there peacefully, only gently flipping their tails to keep the flies off.

I went over to the one named Whisper – remembering our mother's secret society, the Whispers, and hoping it was a good omen. "Hello," I said nervously. She put out her nose and nuzzled my hand. Well, that seemed a good start.

The stable girl was apparently known as Emma Two due to there being several Emmas. She led our horses over to the mounting block and then pulled sugar cubes out of her pocket to keep them occupied. "Up you get," she said to us with a toothy grin.

I took a deep breath and climbed the small steps up on to the block. My palms were sweating. *Getting on a horse is nothing*, I tried to tell myself. *Yes, but it's staying on that's the hard part*, my mind insisted.

I looked over at Scarlet for reassurance, but she was chewing her fingernails and pointedly looking anywhere other than at the horses. No help there.

"You remember how to do it?" Emma Two asked in her

singsong accent. Seeing my expression, she put her hand in the stirrup. "Just stick your foot here, put your weight on it and then throw your leg over the other side. And make sure you end up facing the right way."

I tensed my muscles... and did as she said. My foot seemed to swing over the horse all on its own. I waited several seconds before I dared to open my eyes. I was the right way round, at least. I slid my foot into the other stirrup.

I'd done it! I was on!

Whisper took a few steps forward, and I gripped the reins.

"Whoa, there," Emma Two said, her toothy smile making another appearance. "Keep calm. If you're fine, she's fine."

I swallowed and tried to tell myself I was definitely fine. But I had to move. I couldn't stay stationary by the mounting block – Scarlet needed to get on too, for one thing.

Steadying myself, I tried to remember what I'd done when pony trekking in the past. I gave Whisper the gentlest squeeze I could manage, and she walked off across the yard. She came to a halt beside a water trough and began having a drink. I had successfully led my horse to water. Well, that was something.

"Are you from around here?" I heard Scarlet ask Emma Two. I got the impression she was stalling.

"Oh yes," the stable girl said. "I was born here. I live on a farm down the way."

Scarlet said nothing for a moment. And then she said: "So you know the story? About the lake, and the village? Is it true?"

My horse pulled her head up, water dripping from her mouth, and I remembered to pull the rein to turn her round. Now I was back facing my twin again.

"It's all true," Emma said. She patted Shadow on the nose. "It wasn't so long ago. My ma was still young, but my nanna remembers it well. Our farm is up on the hill, so they didn't have to move, but they lost the village."

Scarlet put a tentative hand on the saddle. "What about the stories about restless spirits?"

Emma Two's expression darkened a little. "Nanna doesn't like to talk about that."

Scarlet looked at me. I shrugged. I wasn't sure what that meant.

My twin couldn't stall any longer. I watched as she swung herself on to the horse in much the same worried and undignified way that I'd done. "I did it!" she said. I grinned at her.

I think we both felt like we were managing really well – at least until we looked around, and saw that Ariadne was already doing laps of the yard.

* * *

When everyone had a horse, Mrs Hunt called out a few instructions and then took the lead, trotting off out to the main driveway. People followed her, some looking totally at ease, others (like Scarlet and me) taking it more slowly.

There was misty rain in the air, but at least it cooled things a bit, and seemed to make the horses more alert. Whisper went forward quickly, eager to follow the others, her ears pricked. I just tried to sit back and let her do what she wanted. She seemed to know what she was doing.

Even Rose was riding – I knew how much she loved horses and ponies, but I'd never actually seen her on one. She looked totally at home, and she trotted ahead of us, rising and falling in the saddle. Elsie and Cassandra shared a glance as she passed.

Scarlet was beside me. She looked a little green.

"Are you all right?" I asked.

"It's high up," she said, gripping her reins.

I had to agree with her. I was attempting to not look at the ground – it didn't help that the rain was starting to make it slippery, and the horses' hooves were skidding on the wet ground. Mrs Hunt had reminded us to keep our heels back in the stirrups to help us stay balanced, but mine kept slipping forward.

"Couldn't she go a bit slower?" Scarlet muttered. Mrs

Hunt was already getting ahead of everyone as she went down the hill.

"Come on!" she shouted to everyone, waving her riding crop at us. "We're heading for the trail!"

Ariadne trotted up to us. "Isn't mine lovely? His name is Rusty!" She patted his rust-coloured coat.

"Same word I'd use to describe my riding skills," Scarlet said grumpily.

We followed Mrs Hunt. Riding downhill was even worse than on the flat. I kept thinking Whisper was going to slip and fall over. The road led down to the lake, but rather than continuing along, the riding instructor took a trail that led off into the forest. I shared a worried look with Scarlet.

"Yippee!" Ariadne cried, trotting past us towards the trees. She still had her camera round her neck, which didn't seem like a brilliant idea, but she was enjoying herself so much that I didn't want to say anything.

We entered the forest, and it was almost like a different world. The canopy of trees sheltered us from the rain, and the scent of pine was stronger than ever. The trail led through an endless sea of green, well worn by the hooves of horses that had walked it before. I started to relax a little. The ground wasn't too steep, and the horses were calm, crunching gently through the undergrowth.

The trail seemed to be leading round the lake, because every so often I caught a glimpse of the water shining through the trees. I wondered if it led anywhere, or if we were just going to go all the way round.

My question was answered when we came to a clearing in the forest. There was an enormous rock in the centre that looked as if it had been casually tossed there by a giant.

"Don't forget to tug on your reins to stop!" Mrs Hunt called out as Anna sped past the clearing and had to turn round and come back again. "Not too hard!" she added. Cassandra had pulled up on her reins so hard that she had almost tipped over backwards.

Scarlet and I thankfully managed to get our horses to stop with some gentle tugging. They began trying to nibble at what little grass there was on the forest floor.

"Right," Mrs Hunt said. "This is Goliath's Rock. Many thousands of years old, we think. Probably left here by a glacier."

"Ooh, ooh!" said Ariadne, raising her hand. "It's called an 'erratic'!"

"How did you even know that?" Scarlet asked her.

Ariadne shrugged happily.

Mrs Hunt smiled a tight smile. "Right, a good place for a brief stop, but n—"

BANG!

Before I even knew what was happening, birds were shooting upwards from the treetops, and Mrs Knight's black horse had reared. I watched in horror as her saddle slipped and she went tumbling off.

And suddenly the horses were running, scattering into the woods, and all I could do was hang on for dear life...

Chapter Twenty-six

SCARLET

"Ivy!" I cried after my sister. My horse was running, the wind in her mane, away from the others, away from the noise. Ivy's horse was heading in the other direction.

"Oh God, oh God..." I panicked as Shadow sped away from the group. I tried with all my might to stay on, clinging tightly to the reins. I tugged at them, but the horse wasn't listening. She raced on, ears back against her head. The rain whipped my face. A branch came up at speed and I had to lie almost flat against the saddle to stop it knocking me off.

I peered up again, my heart beating a thousand miles an hour, and saw an enormous log lying across the ground. I realised that if I didn't stop, we were going to jump it. "No! Shadow, no!" I called out.

We got nearer and nearer to the log and I felt as though my heart was going to fall out of my mouth. I tugged on the reins as hard as I could.

And, at the last second, the horse swerved.

She halted, snorting, her breath making clouds in the air.

I tipped forward, desperately trying to calm my painful lungs. Eventually, I could breathe normally again. I sat up, and looked around.

I had no idea where I was.

"Oh, for goodness' sake," I said to no one. I was lost and alone, stuck on a frightened horse.

What on earth had just happened? That sudden loud noise had come out of nowhere, and spooked all the horses. It was almost like a gunshot. Somebody shooting game, or rabbits, maybe? But it had sounded so close... And Mrs Knight... Oh no, Mrs Knight... And Ivy...

I turned in the saddle. "Ivy!" I yelled again. "Someone! Can anyone hear me?"

A bird took flight at my voice and flapped away across the sky. The rain fell more and more heavily, until it was coming through the trees. It splashed on to my helmet.

"Ivy!" I tried, louder.

There was a loud rustling, and I pulled on the reins to turn towards it. I prayed it wasn't a shotgun-wielding maniac who I had just alerted to my presence.

"Scarlet!" I heard.

A horse came through the trees, but the rider wasn't Ivy – it was Ariadne.

"Scarlet!" she said again, trotting closer. "Are you all right?"

"I'm alive! But very lost!" I looked around. I couldn't see anything that gave away what direction I'd come from. The ground was so covered with pine needles that I couldn't even see any footprints.

"Me too," Ariadne replied. "Thank goodness I found you." She patted Rusty and muttered in his ear while he nibbled at some leaves.

I adjusted my helmet, which was threatening to fall off. "Did you see where Ivy went?"

Ariadne shook her head. "I saw Mrs Knight's horse get spooked, and then everything just happened so fast." She stared at the ground. "Oh! Remember what Mrs Moss said? Go downhill if you get lost?"

She pointed, and I saw what she meant. The ground was gently sloping downhill, which hopefully meant the lake was in that direction. I took a deep breath. "Right, brilliant,

Ariadne. You're a genius." I usually proclaimed her to be a genius with a lot more enthusiasm, but I was too worried at that moment. What had happened to everyone?

Ariadne turned her horse and began to tread the sloping ground through the forest. Reluctantly, I gave Shadow a squeeze with my heels and she lifted her head back up. Seeing Rusty trot off through the trees, she seemed to get the idea that she was supposed to follow.

Everything looked the same. Trees, trees and more trees. I wasn't sure if the ground was even sloping down-wards any more. "Are you certain this is right?" I called to Ariadne.

"I have no idea!" she called back.

But suddenly, I saw it in the distance – the silver glimmer of rippling water. "There! The lake!"

We headed towards it, and soon we were emerging from the trees and out on to the road that ringed the lake. There was a gentle shore with a bench on it. Shadow came to a halt as we neared the water. I hoped she didn't fancy taking a dip.

The sky was growing darker, almost like it was evening rather than the middle of the day. That strange, unsettled energy was still in the air, and there was a threatening rumble up above. My clothes were getting soaked, and my eyes were stinging.

"Oh," said Ariadne wistfully. "It's stunning in the rain." She pulled out her camera from her jumper, snapped a photo of the lake with the tower in the distance, and then tucked the camera away again.

"For goodness' sake, Ariadne," I said, "this is not the time for photographs." But before she could reply, I spotted another horse further along the road. "Hello!" I yelled. I waved my arms at the rider, as frantically as I could without alarming our horses.

As they came closer, I saw that it was Nadia. She looked like a drowned rat, and I supposed we probably looked the same.

"Where did everyone go?" she called over. She was definitely a much better rider than I was, and she quickly trotted over and pulled her horse to a neat stop beside us.

"I don't know," I said. "Have you seen Ivy?"

Nadia shook her head. "I thought I saw someone but my horse wouldn't slow down. She was terrified. I tried to stop her, but..." She pulled a face. "At least she seems to be listening to me again now." She gave the horse a half-hearted pat.

Ariadne turned Rusty round and stared back down the road. "The hotel's over there," she said, pointing. "If we head back in that direction, we might be able to see the rock and find the others."

I looked at Nadia, and she shrugged. It was the only plan we had.

We were some way down the road, staring into the forest, when Nadia spotted it. "Through there!"

I squinted through the rain. I thought I could see what she was looking at, but I wasn't sure.

"Is that definitely the rock?" I said.

"Looks like it," said Ariadne, shielding her eyes with one hand.

Reluctantly I urged Shadow into the trees, and we headed towards the boulder. Were we heading back into danger? What if that sound had actually been a gunshot? Or someone deliberately trying to scare the horses?

But still, I pressed on. We had to find Ivy. And what if Mrs Knight was really hurt?

As we neared the rock, I began to hear frantic voices. But what we found wasn't exactly what I'd expected.

Mrs Knight was sitting on the ground, her arm in an awkward position and pain etched on her face. Mrs Hunt was kneeling beside her.

I couldn't see Ivy, but some of the others were back. They'd climbed off their horses and left them tied to branches. And they were all standing round Rose, backing her against the rock. She was shaking her head. I couldn't tell if it was rain or tears on her cheeks.

"Hey!" I yelled. "Get away from her!"

But either they weren't listening or they couldn't hear me over the rain.

"You did this!" Elsie was screaming. "You did something to the horses, didn't you! Mrs Knight's saddle shouldn't have slipped like that!"

Rose was just mouthing *No* silently, over and over. I had to help her. But to do that, I needed to get off the stupid horse.

"You probably scared them yourself, you freak!" That was Cassandra.

"She's possessed!"

"She's crazy!"

I peered at the ground. It seemed a long way down. It was rocky and the mud was all churned up – not exactly a nice landing. I tried to remember what I'd been taught, but I was cold and wet and my mind wasn't cooperating. In the end I just swung my leg up and tipped downwards awkwardly, bruising my chest in the process. *Oof*.

I should've tied Shadow up, I knew that, but there was no time. I left her reins dangling and threw them to Ariadne as I ran over to the rock.

"Hey!" I wasn't going to waste any time talking. I grabbed the back of Elsie's jumper and pulled her backwards.

She spun round and shoved me in the chest, knocking the air out of my lungs even more. "Don't touch me!" she yelled.

"I told you to leave Rose alone!" I gasped. "And I MEANT IT!" I shoved her back, and she went sprawling into the mud.

The sky rumbled with thunder again, and I knew how it felt. This was the last straw. I went to hit Elsie, but Cassandra grabbed my arm and twisted it back, and another girl tried to take hold of my legs.

I shook them off furiously and darted backwards. Rose was still pressed against the rock, sobbing. I stood beside her, panting to get my breath back.

"She has nothing to do with this!" I yelled at them through the rain. "It was just an accident!"

"*She* gave Mrs Knight that horse!" Cassandra insisted. "And now her arm is probably broken! That lunatic should NEVER have been allowed on this trip!"

I glanced worriedly back across the clearing at Mrs Knight. At least Mrs Hunt was helping her, but it meant neither of them had noticed what was going on. "Well, Rose didn't spook the horses, did she?" I shot back. "She was right here with us!"

"I don't know what she did," said Elsie, taking a

threatening step forward. "But we're not letting her get away with it this time."

"You'll have to get past me first, you cowards!" I looked at the other girls, who were standing around not saying anything. They may not have been attacking Rose, but they certainly weren't stopping the others from doing it.

But Elsie was different. She dived for me and threw me out of the way, and this time it was me who landed in the mud, my helmet cracking on a rock as I went down.

I tried to scramble up, spluttering and furious, but my head swam, and the mud sucked me in, and the scene whirled in front of my eyes...

"Scarlet!" I heard Ariadne yell.

I watched Elsie and Cassandra grabbing Rose by the arms, pulling on them until her face crumpled with pain. She struggled and I could see she wanted to cry out, to get the teachers' attention... but her voice failed her.

"Hey," Elsie said slowly and cruelly. "She wouldn't show us her necklace before. Why don't we make her show us?"

She reached out, but that was when Rose let loose a scream so ear-piercing that Elsie and Cassandra dropped her and clapped their hands over their ears.

Then a brilliant white flash split the sky in two.

And as I lay in the mud, Rose ran headlong into the rain without looking back.

Chapter Twenty-seven

Ivy

'd been riding in circles for what felt like forever, alone and afraid as the rain fell and the sky thundered overhead.

I was just beginning to lose hope when I thought I spotted a familiar rock through the trees. I pointed Whisper towards it and hoped for the best. She seemed reluctant to head back there, pulling up on her reins and flattening her ears. I didn't blame her. Especially when I heard the scream.

It was horrible. Blood-curdling, even. It sounded almost inhuman.

And then a flash of lightning lit up the sky, turning everything white.

Whisper whinnied nervously. I was shaking and almost couldn't breathe. Something was very wrong. What if it was Scarlet? Or one of my friends? I urged Whisper on faster, and soon we emerged back into the clearing beside the rock.

Scarlet was lying on the ground, struggling to get up, Ariadne and Nadia kneeling down beside her. A group of girls stood nearby, yelling at each other. Mrs Knight was sitting on the other side of the clearing with Mrs Hunt, and her face was pale and drawn, her arm clutched to her chest.

I didn't know what to do. It was too much to take in.

Scarlet.

Without even thinking, I jumped off the horse. It was a long way down, and my legs slammed into the ground, so that I had to bend them to absorb the shock. I ran towards my twin, the rain pounding around me.

"Scarlet! What happened?"

She looked up at me, gasping. "I'm fine," she said. "Just a bit winded. Helmet took a hit." She sat up. "I couldn't... I couldn't save her..."

"Save who?" I looked up at Ariadne and Nadia desperately.

"They grabbed your friend Rose," Nadia said. "And then she screamed and ran away."

Rose had made that sound? I could barely believe it. "What did they do to her?"

"They hurt her and tried to take her necklace," Ariadne said, her voice shaking.

Suddenly, all the fear and panic that had been building inside me turned into something else. It was like a burning sensation, starting from my heart and spreading through my skin.

The old Ivy would have run, or cried, or hidden. But I wasn't that person any more. I had become something so much greater than that. Instead of turning my anger inwards, I channelled it, and used it.

As Ariadne helped Scarlet up, I marched over to the rock, and climbed up on to the lower part of it, beside the group of girls yelling at each other about Rose.

"What was that scream?"

"Did she do that? Make the lightning happen?"

"We should go after her!"

"ALL OF YOU, SHUT UP RIGHT NOW AND LISTEN!"

The rabble descended into stunned silence, until there was nothing but the wind and the rain and the horses' snorting breaths and stamping hooves.

"You're all *despicable*!" I yelled. "You've bullied a frightened girl and chased her off into a *storm*! And hurt my sister for trying to defend her! All while our headmistress is injured and needs our help!"

"But—" Cassandra started.

I pointed at her. "I don't want to hear one word from you, Cassandra! All of you should be ashamed of yourselves. We need to help Mrs Knight and find Rose and get inside!"

I didn't know how we were going to find Rose, or where she might have gone, but at least she wasn't injured. I jumped down off the rock and was amazed to see everyone running over to Mrs Knight. What I'd said had worked!

I bent forward, catching my breath. "That... was amazing..." Scarlet said.

"No time for that," I said. "We're in danger out here. You saw the lightning! And not just that, whatever scared the horses..."

"You're right," said Ariadne.

Helping Scarlet, we hurried back over to Mrs Knight. Mrs Hunt was helping her up. "I'm certain her arm's broken, girls. We need to get back."

"Are you all right, Miss?" Elsie asked, her simpering tone returning.

"Oh, so now she cares?" Scarlet muttered.

"I'm... fine..." Mrs Knight managed, but her face said otherwise. "Is... everyone... here?"

A few more girls appeared through the trees on horseback, but I wasn't sure if everyone had returned yet.

Mrs Hunt decided to take charge. "If you can get on your horse, do it. If you can't, lead them back. Someone take Mrs Knight's horse, please. We'll just have to hope that everyone has the sense to go towards the hotel. We need to move quickly now."

The rain pounded on my helmet. I was soaked through and shivering, the warmth of my anger starting to wear off. It seemed like the clouds were endless, pouring their contents into the valley.

"But Rose..." I started to say.

Another flash lit up the sky, and we heard the unmistakable *crack* of a splitting tree trunk.

There was no time. We had to get to safety.

I'd managed to climb back on to Whisper with help from Ariadne, and Scarlet got on behind me. Ariadne raced along beside us, leading Shadow by the reins. All of us sped through the driving rain, the horses' hooves clicking on the road. I was clinging on desperately, not wanting to go fast, but wanting even less to be out in the storm. Scarlet was clinging on even more desperately to me.

The horses seemed to know where they were going, sensing the way out of danger. I was terrified that they would slip on the wet hill, but Whisper managed to keep her footing as she followed the others. Mrs Knight was on the back of Mrs Hunt's horse, holding tightly, her other arm still clutched to her chest.

Soon the hotel was in sight, but I couldn't breathe a sigh of relief just yet. There was another roar of thunder and flash of lightning, merely moments apart. Some of the horses broke away, but everyone managed to rein them back in again.

Rose is still out there, I reminded myself. I just prayed that she would hide somewhere safe and then find her way back to the hotel.

Finally, we came up on to the driveway, the gravel spraying from beneath the horses' hooves. I saw the stable girls anxiously waiting for us beneath the eaves of the stables.

"Girls!" Mrs Hunt cried out. "We need help! See if you can find a doctor! Help these girls off and get the horses safely away!"

There was a flurry of nods and "Yes, Miss"es, and the girls got to work. One of the Emmas ran for the hotel.

I managed to pull Whisper to a halt, but as Scarlet and I ungracefully dismounted, the horse headed straight for an open stall to get in the warm and dry. I didn't blame her one bit.

Miss Bowler came charging out of the hotel like a cannonball. "GIRLS!" she boomed. "WHAT'S GOING ON?"

She caught sight of Mrs Hunt helping Mrs Knight off the

horse, and thudded over. Soon she was helping Mrs Knight shuffle inside. I gulped at the sight of the headmistress's arm. It really didn't look good.

"Do you think Rose will come back?" Ariadne said as we hurried for cover.

"She will," Scarlet said. Always the confident one.

But as another lightning strike washed the sky, I began to feel more and more afraid.

Warmth. That was the first thing I felt as we all huddled inside the hotel reception area. It was warm and dry, a fire roaring in the hearth. We all collapsed in a heap, drenched and dripping.

"What is the meaning of this?" I heard Mr Rudge demand. He marched out of the door to the office. "You can't just come in here all—"

"We will come in here however we like, my good man!" Miss Bowler boomed. "We have an injury here!"

Mr Rudge looked like he was about to argue, but then his wife appeared, accompanied by the man with the monocle and the walrus moustache. "This is Dr Davies," she said. "He's retired, but he can take a look at you."

Mrs Knight smiled, weakly but gratefully, as the doctor took her away, Miss Bowler and Mrs Hunt trailing behind them.

As we sat, leaning against each other, feeling exhausted,

I saw Phyllis walking in. She was wearing a fetching green raincoat. "Oh goodness, girls!" she said to the whole group of us. "Caught in the storm?"

Everyone nodded. The rain was battering the windows of the hotel now. I didn't think I'd ever felt so relieved to be inside.

"At least we're going home tomorrow," said Nadia wearily.

"What?" said Phyllis. Her face slipped into a frown. "You are?"

She seemed disappointed, but I had no idea why. Did she enjoy our company so much?

"I just... I'd hoped I'd have more time to get to know you all!" she said. "And to teach you some more orienteering. I don't get students often." She smiled sadly. "Well... it was nice to meet you."

She turned as if she were about to leave, but walked into Miss Bowler coming back into the reception area.

Miss Bowler started counting everyone. "Are we all here?"

I stood up. "No, Miss. People were picking on Rose and she ran off..."

Miss Bowler froze in her counting. She looked like she was about to explode. "WHAT? SHE'S STILL OUT THERE?"

Phyllis stopped in her tracks and turned, looking worried.

239

Scarlet and Ariadne scrambled up beside me as well. "We'll go and look for her, Miss!" Scarlet said.

"No, you will not!" said Miss Bowler. She grabbed a hooded raincoat similar to Phyllis's from a hook on the wall. "Right, I need to go out there..." She looked through the window just as another flash of lightning tore across the sky. I gasped and Ariadne flinched.

"I'll help you search for her!" Phyllis said. "If we split up we can cover more ground. I'm sure I can track her down."

"Right, right," Miss Bowler muttered. "Let's go. No time to waste!"

And then they were both out of the door of the Shady Pines Hotel, and into the oncoming storm.

"I hope they find her," Ariadne whispered. There was a tear rolling down her cheek.

"They will," Scarlet said decisively.

I didn't feel so certain. In fact, deep down, I was very afraid.

Chapter Twenty-eight

SCARLET

I may have seemed confident on the surface, but beneath I was starting to panic. I tried not to, but every time I looked out of the window I saw Rose drowning or trapped under a rock or struck by lightning, and my heart started pounding in my chest.

She'll be fine, I kept telling myself. *Miss Bowler and Phyllis will find her.* I said it to the others too. I hoped if I could convince them that I could convince myself.

We couldn't stay in our drenched clothes, so we went up

to our room and got changed. Ariadne fretted about her camera being wet, but she'd had it underneath her jumper and she didn't think the water had got into the mechanism.

I decided that the best thing we could do was to light a fire, so I went and found some logs from one of the fireplaces downstairs. I wasn't sure if that was stealing or not, but since nobody was using them at the time, it seemed a good idea. It was mad how quickly the weather had turned. The sky outside was as dark as night-time.

Ivy and Ariadne were sitting shivering in our room when I returned with an armful of logs. I set them down on the carpet.

"Where did you get those?" Ivy asked.

"Doesn't matter," I replied. I got down on my knees beside the draughty fireplace. It was a little dusty, and didn't look as if it had been used recently.

I stuck my head in to peer up the chimney and check it was clear, but I lost my balance and fell forward...

Through the fireplace.

I sat up. I'd fallen past the grate, and through the board at the back of the fireplace that had looked as though it was solid.

"Scarlet!?"

"Scarlet, what happened?"

That was a good question. I looked around. "I seem to be in the fireplace," I said.

Ivy's concerned face appeared in front of me. "Are you hurt?"

I peered out at her. "No, but... what *is* this?"

I seemed to be in some sort of crawl space, sitting on the board. It was dark, and chilly, and smelt of soot. The walls were rough stone under my hands. But it was quite big – I could move my arms, and there was space above my head.

"Can you see anything?" Ivy asked.

"Not really – hand me a candle?" I stuck my arm back out.

She lit one and gave it to me, and pulling it back in, I used it to illuminate the small space in both directions.

"I think it's a secret passageway!" I hissed out at them.

"What?" I heard Ariadne say. "Really?"

But now I was entranced. This had to mean something. Holding the candle out in front of me, I crept forward through the dust. I could feel the draught now, and I swore I could feel a few spots of rain dripping down on me. As I looked up, I could see that the chimney rose above my head, with a cap on the top to keep most of the rain and the birds out.

I crept a little further, hearing Ivy calling behind me, but her voice faded away into nothingness. I felt like something

243

was drawing me on. I just kept going forward, and soon I noticed another board like the one I had just fallen through. That would be the fireplace of the next room, I guessed. I put my hand on it and felt it wobble slightly. If I'd pushed it or moved it aside, I could've got into the room easily.

A realisation began to dawn on me. Whoever had been trashing the rooms, stealing things, writing words on the walls... they could have easily got around unseen this way. But did that mean it was someone from inside the hotel, or was there another route into this passageway?

I kept going, past more fireplaces, trying not to breathe in too much dust. And then, eventually, I came to the very end. I held the candle up and I saw... *a ladder*. It went upwards into the darkness.

To the roof, I thought. That had to be it. If there was a ladder on the outside of the hotel as well, then someone could easily get up there and then climb back down. Or perhaps somewhere else there was a passage that led down to the basement... There were any number of ways someone could sneak in and 'haunt' the place.

I had to turn back. I squeezed myself into the end of the passage so I could twist round and crawl back to where I'd come from. I emerged from the fireplace, coughing, and handed the candle to Ivy, who was waiting anxiously.

"Where did you go?" she said.

I pointed as I tried to brush some of the soot off my clean dress. "I crawled along it. It goes to the other rooms, and there's a ladder to the roof. I think we've found how our ghost is getting in here."

"So it wasn't Rose," Ariadne said. "It was never Rose." She sat on the bed, and I wondered from the look on her face if she felt guilty. I think she'd had her doubts as well.

I felt the fire swell inside me. None of this was Rose's fault, and now she was in danger. And we were supposed to just sit here and not help? This wasn't right.

"We have to do something," I said. "We have to find Rose, and we have to work out who's doing all of this. What if they get to Rose before we do?"

"Miss Bowler and Phyllis might come back with her, mightn't they?" Ariadne said, her face contorted with worry. She fiddled with the controls on her camera nervously.

"They might," Ivy agreed. "We should wait for them to come back, at least."

I stood up and slammed my fist into the fireplace. "We can't just do nothing! There must be something!"

Ariadne suddenly looked up. "My camera..." she said.

"What about your camera?" I snapped. It was wrong of me, I know, but I was so frustrated. I felt like a coiled spring, and I was fed up with her obsession.

She didn't seem to notice how sharp I'd been. "I've taken lots of pictures," she said. "Around the hotel and the lake. Perhaps we should take á closer look? We might be able to see something that could help us..."

"I don't see what good it will do," I muttered. I longed to run, to do *something*.

"Scarlet," Ivy chastised. "Ariadne's right. We should look. We don't have anything else to go on."

Hurriedly, Ariadne pulled out the little stack of photographs that she'd developed. She even retrieved a magnifying glass from her convoy of suitcases. Then she spread the pictures out all over the bed, and I watched as she and Ivy pored over them. I stood, arms folded, the anger still burning on my skin.

"Hmm," I heard Ariadne say. She started picking up some of her photos of the lake, and putting them in a line. "Look at these," she said suddenly.

That pricked up my interest. Had she really found something? I leant closer.

"There's someone crossing the lake," she said, the familiar excitement back on her face. "Look, in the distance! Heading for the tower!"

I grabbed the magnifying glass off her and peered closer. She was right! There *was* someone there, and not in one of the hotel's rowing boats either. It looked like some sort of canoe.

Ivy leant in and had a look too. "It's a man, I think," she said. "He's got a man's hat on."

"I've not seen any of the men in the hotel wearing a hat like that," I mused.

"It could be someone who lives nearby, couldn't it?" Ariadne asked. "Going fishing or something?"

I held the magnifying glass over it again. "There's no equipment or anything in the boat that I can see. And he's definitely heading right for the tower."

Ivy picked up another photograph from the bed. "I thought I could see something in this one too. I think there's a man there." It was a photograph of all of us, standing around by the woods, and someone appeared to be watching us from the bushes. Just a tall shadow, and a glint of glass. I shuddered at the thought of it. It gave me the creeps.

"I bet it's the same person." I frowned at the picture. "Some freak who lives nearby and wants to spy on the guests."

"We don't know anyone from outside the hotel, though," Ivy began. "Except..."

We all said it at the same time: *"Bob Owens!"*

Chapter Twenty-nine

Ivy

"Oh my goodness," Ariadne said, backing against the bed. "That could be it! He was the one who told us the story about the village and the restless spirits. And I think he had a hat in his bag when we first met him."

She was right! I remembered seeing it fall on the ground.

"And he didn't seem to like the hotel very much, did he?" Scarlet pointed out. The idea had gripped her now, I could tell, and she was going to run with it. "Let's say it was him. He wants to scare people away from the hotel. So he tells

248

everyone this ghost story and makes scary things happen. He could be behind everything!"

"But *why*?" I asked. I felt a little lightheaded. "Why do it? Whoever it is seems to be targeting us."

"Perhaps he's just angry," Ariadne suggested, putting down her magnifying glass. "Perhaps he was around when the village was destroyed. The way he talked about it... it was like he really loved the place. That could be enough to drive someone to revenge."

I remembered what Emma from the stables had said. "It wasn't that long ago, apparently. He's definitely old enough to have been there."

Scarlet snapped her fingers. "And we know how he could get into the hotel at night – the secret passageway."

"But how did he get hold of the relics from the church?" I asked. "I can't imagine he stole them and kept them this whole time. They really looked like they'd come from the bottom of the lake..."

Scarlet wrinkled her nose, annoyed that I found a flaw in her theory. "I don't know," she admitted. "But if it is him, we need to find out, and we need to stop him before someone gets seriously hurt. What if it was him that scared the horses earlier?"

Ariadne clapped her hands to her mouth, horrified. "Someone could have died!"

"Exactly." My twin had a determined expression on her face now. "We need to look for him, and now –" she tapped the photograph of the tower – "we know where to look. Ariadne – I take back what I said about your pictures. Remind me never to doubt your genius!"

Ariadne beamed, but I was beginning to realise that there was a big flaw in this plan. Sheets of water were pouring down the window, and the thunder rumbled overhead, followed by a blinding flash and a deafening *crack*. "Scarlet... I don't see how we can do this. The storm's showing no signs of stopping! If anything it's getting worse, and we have to go home tomorrow."

"Drat!" Scarlet slammed her fist on to the bed. "We'll tell the teachers, then. Or we'll tell the Rudges. We have to do *something*!"

We went back down to the ground floor, armed with our new knowledge and prepared to do something about it. But things suddenly took a turn for the worse.

As we walked into the reception area, Miss Bowler stumbled in through the front door, soaked everywhere that wasn't covered by the raincoat, and deadly pale. One of the stable girls dashed in behind her.

"Miss!" Scarlet ran over. "Did you find Rose?"

Miss Bowler shook her head, droplets of water flying

from her hair as if she were a wet dog. "No sign," she huffed. "And I lost that Moss woman too. I need to speak to the headmistress." She pushed past us, while the stable girl ran up to Mr Rudge at the front desk.

"Sir! The lightning struck a tree and it fell down and the bridge is blocked!" She panted.

"What?" Mr Rudge snapped. "Oh, for goodness' sake..." He dashed away, presumably to look out of the window.

Ariadne looked frantic. "They didn't find Rose or Phyllis! What if Bob Owens has got to them? Or they're trapped somewhere?"

I felt her fear. It was definitely not safe out there, Bob Owens or no Bob Owens. The roar of the storm was louder than ever, the wind and rain battering at the windows. And the lightning... "If we can't cross the bridge..." I said, "we're trapped here."

"We need to hear what Miss Bowler has to say," Scarlet said suddenly, running off along the corridor. I agreed. Grabbing Ariadne's hand, we dashed along behind her until we reached the room where the doctor was bandaging Mrs Knight's arm, and peered round the doorframe.

"My good woman," the doctor was saying to Miss Bowler, waving at Mrs Knight who was lying on a *chaise longue*. "This lady needs rest..."

"Don't you *my good woman* me!" Miss Bowler boomed

at him. She was so loud that his moustache quivered. "This is important!" She turned back to Mrs Knight. "Helena, there's no sign of the girl, nor of that Mrs Moss. It's hellish out there. We need to send out a search party, you need a hospital and then we need to get everyone on the bus and back to Rookwood!"

Mrs Knight looked drained, but a little better, though she paled at this news. "Perhaps that would be best, Eunice," she started.

Scarlet barged in, all thoughts of being stealthy forgotten. "Miss, you can't! They just said that a tree has fallen and the bridge is blocked!"

Miss Bowler whirled round. "No eavesdropping, Grey!" Then she paused, apparently taking in what Scarlet had just said. "Are you sure, girl?"

"Yes," she said, folding her arms indignantly. "Ask Mr Rudge if you don't believe me."

Mrs Knight frowned. "We'll have to stay here until they can clear it," she said weakly.

Miss Bowler was red in the face and still dripping. "I don't fancy spending another night in this place!"

"Neither do I," Mrs Knight admitted. She winced as the doctor folded her arm into a sling. "But we don't have a choice."

"And the missing girl?" Miss Bowler huffed.

"You can't just leave her out there!" Scarlet shouted at them.

Mrs Knight thought about it. "See if you can find anyone willing to help search," she said quietly to Miss Bowler. "Perhaps some of the local people and hotel staff. Keep all the other girls inside. We'll do what we can."

I decided I had to step in. "Miss, the local people... we think Mr Owens might be—"

"GET OUT, BOTH OF YOU!" Miss Bowler yelled. "NOT YOUR BUSINESS! BACK TO YOUR ROOM, NOW!"

And with that, she marched us out of the room and slammed the door in our faces.

"They have to let us look for Rose," Scarlet said as we walked back through the corridors.

"Not a chance," I said. "They don't want us to leave." And I didn't blame them. The hotel was a huge, old, solid building, but I was still half afraid that the storm was going to blow the windows in at any moment. I'd never seen such awful weather.

"Maybe she'll be all right," Ariadne said. "She could just be hiding. Perhaps she found the caves again."

"Well, she can't leave the area around the lake," I said. "The road is blocked." I wasn't sure if that was a reassuring thought or not.

"Let's go and see," Scarlet said, and she dragged us both off towards the restaurant, which had the best view of the lake on the ground floor.

Mr and Mrs Rudge were standing there together, staring out of the window at the storm. He looked as though he was about to tear his hair out. "How are our customers going to get here with this?" he said, gesturing down at the bridge.

We sneaked over to the big windows and looked out at where he was pointing. You could see where the huge tree was blocking the road, the trunk split and smoking.

You'd need something big to lift it, or a lot of men to saw it up, and that wasn't going to happen in the middle of a storm.

"Really, Gerald?" Mrs Rudge snapped. "That's all you're worried about?" She ripped off her apron and threw it on the floor.

"What?" Mr Rudge called after her as she left. "What did I say?"

"That's not good," I said.

"Oh my gosh!" Ariadne exclaimed suddenly. "Look!"

In the midst of the storm, someone was rowing a boat across the lake again. It was hard to make out from this distance, but it looked a lot like the one in Ariadne's picture, like a canoe rather than like the rowing boats we'd rented that bobbed by the shore. I couldn't see who was paddling it, or make out any more detail. It was little more than a black blob on the water, but it was definitely a boat.

"What if that's him?" Ariadne said, her eyes wide. "Bob Owens?"

Scarlet turned away from the window. "And what if he's got Rose? Why else would he be out in this? He's up to something, I know it!"

And before I could talk her out of it, Scarlet was running for the reception area. A row of raincoats was hanging there, presumably belonging to the Rudges or the other guests. She grabbed one and pulled it on, though it was too big for her.

"Scarlet, you can't," I said. "That doesn't belong to you. And it's not safe!"

"You heard what the teachers said!" Ariadne whimpered. "We need to stay inside."

Scarlet grabbed two more of the coats off the hooks and thrust them into our arms. "I wouldn't leave you behind," she said, "and I'm not leaving her behind either."

"I want to rescue her as much as you do! But what if we just put ourselves in danger and can't even find her?" I couldn't believe Scarlet would do something so reckless.

Actually, I definitely could, but that was beside the point.

"It's just a storm," said Scarlet. "We'll get a bit wet and cold, maybe." She saw my disbelieving expression. "I've had worse, Ivy. *Much* worse. But Rose is out there, and she's probably terrified, and maybe someone's taken her. Maybe he's locking her up in that tower right now. Are you going to just stand here and let that happen?"

I could see the fear behind my twin's anger. Someone had taken her and imprisoned her, and if there was the smallest chance it could happen to anyone else... She couldn't risk that. I understood.

And Rose... There was no one to care for her. Just like we'd thought there was no one to care for us. We now knew that wasn't true for us, but what about her? Without Violet, she was alone in the world.

Unless she had us.

"All right," I whispered.

Ariadne looked at me, and the second our eyes met, I knew she was going to come too. We stuck together. No questions.

We put the raincoats on. The rain hammered down, the lightning flashed, and my heart raced. Determined, Scarlet wrenched open the front door of the hotel.

And we set out into the storm.

Chapter Thirty

SCARLET

It was worse than it had been earlier, if that was possible. The falling rain felt like knives, driving downwards. The clouds looked like they were boiling in the black sky. I could barely see.

But was I going to let that stop me? No, I blooming well wasn't.

I ran down the hill outside the hotel, Ivy and Ariadne yelling after me to slow down, my feet splashing through puddles and skidding on the wet ground. The air smelt damp and earthy, but it was full of electricity too, almost sizzling. The hairs on the back of my neck were standing up.

We have to get across the lake. We have to see what's in that tower. We have to find Rose. The thoughts ran through my head over and over.

We got down to the lakeside and the little jetty, where the rowing boats were being battered by the rain.

"Are you sure this is safe?" Ivy shouted over the noise of the rain.

"No!" I replied, as my feet flew over the wet boards. I knew the boat I wanted. The *Adventure*.

At least it's not the sea, I thought to myself, though even the wind alone was making waves on the lake.

"Come on!" I yelled to the others, waving them on. "Get in!"

Ivy and Ariadne hopped into the boat, shivering. Ariadne slipped off the rope that was tying it to the jetty, and straight away the old thing began to move. I began rowing as hard as I possibly could, the oars cutting through the choppy water.

Since I was rowing backwards, Ariadne had to shout directions at me. "Left! No, the other left! Straight! Keep going!"

"Can you see it?" I tried to turn my neck, but it was hard while I was keeping hold of the oars – not to mention that I was half blind from the rain.

"It's right up ahead!" Ivy threw her arm out. We were getting close to the tower. The second time I turned, I could see it looming up on the shore, surrounded by forest, like something out of a particularly nasty fairy tale.

"Look!" Ariadne said suddenly. "There's the canoe!" So we were right. Whoever it was, Bob Owens or not, they had taken the canoe to the tower.

Soon we were close enough to the tower to touch the base of it. I almost crashed into it, knocking the edge of the boat against the wall and nearly sending us all flying. I stopped rowing and turned to look.

The tower jutted out from the shore a little way – there was a bridge from the land reaching out to it, and the canoe was moored underneath the bridge, neatly hidden out of sight. "Over there," Ivy said, pointing to it. A ladder went up the side of the bridge from the water.

I used my hand to shove the boat away from the wall and then started to row again, until we were next to the ladder. "You two go first!" I yelled to the others.

Ivy looked up at it, unconvinced, but soon she had grabbed hold and was climbing up. I held on to an iron rung on the wall, hoping to keep the boat steady. It was cold and slimy with algae.

Ariadne followed Ivy, heaving herself up and up. Now I was left in the boat. *My turn.* I shivered, watching the rain drip off my hood, trying to work myself up to it. As soon as I let go of the rung, the boat started to wobble and drift away. *Not good.* I picked up the soggy rope from the ground and tied it to the rung using the best knot I could manage, which wasn't good either, but it held it for now.

"We made it!" I heard Ariadne shout.

"Scarlet, are you coming?" That was Ivy.

"Hang on!" I yelled back. I stared up at the ladder as the boat drifted on the water. I took a deep breath... and jumped.

I had hold of the ladder, the rungs as wet and slippery as the one I'd tied the boat to. I began to climb, and tried not to look down.

I came to the top, and reached out a hand to Ivy and Ariadne, who pulled me up over the parapet. We all sat there for a moment on the wet stone, panting, not quite believing we'd done it. Thunder rolled overhead, another flash of white... We had to get inside.

The tower was enormous, seen this close up. Big and black and menacing, with slitted windows and a huge door like an angry mouth.

"Are you sure he's in there?" Ivy asked.

"Someone is," Ariadne pointed out. There was a bolt on the door, but it was slid back.

"Come on," I said, and strode towards the entrance,

sounding braver than I felt. But whoever was waiting for us in there... We could deal with them, I was sure of that.

Do it for Rose, I thought, as I grabbed the handle, heaved open the door and heard... music?

It was some sort of symphony, playing loudly. The sound was crackly, like it was on an old gramophone.

All three of us peered inside, but the darkness gave nothing away. I steeled myself and stepped forward, pulling the others in behind me. Then Ivy tugged the door closed, shutting out the storm.

"At least it's dry in here," Ariadne whispered. The water dripped off our clothes and on to the stone floor.

It was dry, and strangely warm too. The loud music was drowning out the weather outside. If it weren't for the fact we were surrounded by dark stone, I might've called it *homely*.

I could see a light coming from one side of the entranceway, so I headed towards it cautiously. The music got louder as I stepped closer. There was an arch, and it opened on to a round room...

We stepped in, and I couldn't believe the sight that met our eyes.

The room was tall and lit by gas lamps. The air was filled with the music, and the smell of firewood. There was an enormous hearth, with a fire raging in it.

And then there was the furniture. A bed, a table, a huge chest, a washbasin, a hat stand with hats hanging from it.

And then there was the wind-up gramophone, the tinny orchestra swelling out of it, and next to it, an old-fashioned diving suit with a helmet.

And then there was the wall, covered with old photographs of blank-eyed villagers staring at the camera, and newspaper clippings, headlines blaring out:

WATER COMPANY BUYS VILLAGE

VILLAGERS PROTEST
CREATION OF RESERVOIR

CONSTRUCTION BEGINS ON NEW DAM

And there, sitting in a worn armchair in front of the fire, humming along to the music and oblivious to our entrance, was Bob Owens.

With a quick glance at the others, who were wide-eyed in disbelief, I whispered, "Look for Rose!" and then marched in front of Bob. His eyes snapped open.

"Whoa, girl, you startled me." He looked up and his gaze

moved across the three of us. "You two as well. How did you get in here?"

He stood up, sprightly for an old man, and rubbed at his grey hair with a towel.

"Through the front door," I said indignantly, hands on my hips. "Are you going to explain yourself?"

He frowned. "Explain what?"

"Why you're living in a tower? Why you have all this stuff?" I gestured at the newspaper clippings and the diving suit.

"This is my home now," he said. He walked over to the gramophone and stopped the needle, the music skidding to a halt. "It's a straining tower – it removes debris from the water. But this workers' room was left empty, so I moved in." He shrugged. "I didn't want to live in some new soulless place. I wanted to stay in the valley, to be close to my home."

"So you really were one of the people from the village?" Ivy asked as she peered around. "In the story you told?"

"Of course," he said, as if we were slow and had only just caught up. "Born and bred in Seren." He put a proud fist to his chest. "All of us Owenses, going back generations."

Ariadne had tiptoed over to the other side of the room and was standing next to the heavy chest. There was a mighty creak as she opened the lid, and I heard her gasp.

"Hey!" Bob spun round. "What are you doing?"

She reached into the chest and held up a stack of old prayer books, just like the one that had been left dripping with water in the hotel.

"Put those down," he demanded. His face was burning red. "Stop touching my things."

"It *was* you," she said. She put the prayer books down, but then reached into the chest and began pulling out other things – another candlestick, a Communion goblet, a metal cross thick with rust. "You've been leaving these in the hotel!" She looked at the diving suit. It had a weird round helmet and long rubber gloves, and there was a lamp on the top. "Did you dive down and get them? Where did you get this suit?"

"I... I..." He spluttered, going over to her and grabbing all the objects. "I was in the Navy for a while. But that's not your business." He shoved the objects back into the chest and tried to change the subject. "These are my things. From my church. I'm allowed to have them."

"Yes, but you've been scaring people," I said. "On purpose. It's not just these old bits of junk. You're behind all of it, aren't you? The writing on the wall, going through people's things, frightening our horses..."

"Hang on a minute," he said, holding up a finger. "I didn't—"

"Turning on the taps in the night," Ivy added. "Scaring us in the cave. Stealing things."

"Why did you do it?" I asked. "Do you hate the Rudges?" And then I remembered why we were there, and added: "Did you take our friend? Do you know where she is?"

Bob waved his arms. "For goodness' sake, all of you, shut up for a minute and listen, and I'll explain!"

We shut up.

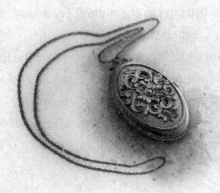

Chapter Thirty-one

IVY

Wearily, Bob traipsed back over to his armchair and sank down into it. "All right," he said, not looking at us, "all right. Here's the thing. You know what the village meant to me. They tore down my home, all of our homes, just to give water to some rich folks in the city. And some of those same rich folks came and opened a bloody hotel. They sat up on the hill and laughed at us. Their lovely *lakeside view*," he spat, "where our homes had once stood."

I started to say something, but he held up a finger. I waited.

"I had a farm," he continued. "It was my family's livelihood. I was raised to be a farmer, and then the land was all sold. What's a farmer without a farm? They paid us off, a pittance, but my ma died and my da drank the money away. He'd lost everything. I went off and joined the Navy because that was all there was left." He pulled down the collar of his shirt a little way to reveal a nasty-looking scar that spread across his chest, before pulling it back up again. "I got that for my troubles."

"Didn't you have any other family?" Ariadne asked gently.

Bob stared into the fire then, as if it might tell him the answer. "I had a sister, and a brother," he said finally. "David. He signed up to help build the dam. Fell right from the top. Killed instantly." He shook his head, the glassy reflection of the fire flickering in his eyes.

There was a long silence, but Ariadne finally broke it. "So you dive down and get the items from the church." She sat down on the stone floor at Bob's feet. "I saw the lights," she said. "Under the lake. That was you, wasn't it? And when my foot was grabbed…"

He didn't answer her, his eyes blank and sparkling with

the reflection of the fire. "Everyone took all they owned from their houses, but the vicar just locked up the church. You should see it down there... it's so grey and still and cold and... *dead*. My sister, Evelyn... she died when she was small, and her grave was there. And now she's under the lake."

An image filled my head. The silent church, locked shut in the strange grey underwater light, rows and rows of graves where no one could ever read them. "But... you got inside the church?" I asked.

He looked at me for the first time, then. "Some of the builders must've smashed the church windows, you see. Thought there was no harm in it since no one would ever see it again." There were deep furrows in his brow. "And the roof fell in under the weight of the water. The place where everyone I knew was christened and married and buried." He shook his head sadly. "The prayer books I rescued beforehand. The rest... I go down there, and I bring bits and pieces back."

I felt the prickle of oncoming tears, but I fought them off. Just because Bob had had a tragic life, it didn't mean it was all right for him to do what he'd done. It was like Miss Fox – she'd been locked up in an asylum when she was younger, and then she'd gone on to try to control everyone else. She wanted to get her own back on the world.

But Scarlet, she'd been through the same, and she hadn't

let it change her. No, that was wrong – she had let it change her, but for the better.

You could fight the world, or you could try to change it.

"I understand," said Scarlet slowly. "I understand why you're angry. But why do all this? You could move on. You could try to stop this happening to others."

I could hear Bob gritting his teeth. "I know." He shook his head. "But they had to know what they'd done to us. I believe what I said about the spirits not being able to rest. I had to be their voice."

"I know you think they're laughing at you," Ariadne said. "But they're not. I promise. They're just trying to make a living, like you were. I don't think you're getting the message across. You're just making everyone scared and upset by what you're doing. You're making the Rudges feel guilty, but they're not even responsible! The people who built the reservoir are responsible!"

Bob shrugged slowly. "None of them are here, are they? The hotel was easy. I knew the ways in. Besides, it was only some old objects, a bit of water and paint. I didn't *hurt* anybody."

"But... the rooms were ransacked," I said. "Things stolen. And someone scared our horses, and our friend is missing..."

Bob's frown changed to one of puzzlement. "That's what

I was trying to tell you. I don't know anything about any of that."

"Really?" Scarlet said. We looked at each other. This wasn't going the way I'd expected.

"I've not seen your friend. I was out until just now, when the storm hit, you know, but I didn't see anyone."

"Are you sure, sir?" Ariadne leant forward. "This is really important. Did you see anything?"

"I heard that loud noise – that's what startled your horses, is it? Thought it must be someone hunting. Good rabbit and deer in these woods." He stood up, brushed himself off, and wandered towards the fire. It was like he was brushing away the thoughts of what had happened to his village, just going back to being plain old Bob Owens. "Heard the horses making a fuss. That's it."

I didn't know what to think. Rose had disappeared in this nightmarish storm, and our number-one suspect knew nothing about it. And he didn't know about the other things that had happened either. So that meant...

There was *someone else*.

Someone else was behind this.

And the more I thought about it, the more it made sense. Bob had been targeting the hotel, but someone else had been targeting *us*. Messing up the rooms, taking the necklace, planting it on Rose...

As Bob stared into the fire, a seed of a thought began to grow in my mind. I whispered to the others: "When we came to the hotel, we were supposed to be in the room that Elsie and Cassandra were given, weren't we? But they moved us because we had Rose as well."

The others nodded. "What's your point?" Scarlet hissed back.

"Someone went through their room," I whispered, "and they must have thought it was ours. They took Cassandra's necklace, but it wasn't what they wanted. Then they went through our room and couldn't find anything, so..."

"They planted the necklace!" Ariadne gasped, putting her hand over her mouth.

Scarlet frowned. "So you're saying... someone is after Rose's locket? Or after Rose?"

"Maybe both," I said. Was someone trying to set her up? But who?

Bob turned round. "You three ought to go," he said. He seemed stern but sad. "Your teachers will be looking for you."

Scarlet walked up to him. "You should tell them, Mr Owens. Tell them what you've told us. We can accuse you of all of it..."

"...but then they won't know the real story," I finished. "They'll just call the police and you'll never get to tell anyone again."

For a moment, I was truly frightened that we'd done the wrong thing – that if we told Bob Owens we were going to accuse him, he would shout at us, or lock us up in the tower, or throw us in the lake.

I think he saw the fear written across my face, because he just sighed and said: "I'm not going to stop you, girls. But maybe I'll think about talking to them. Maybe it is time."

He didn't seem to want to say more after that. I hoped he would think about it. Haunting a hotel wasn't going to bring his family or his home back. He seemed to be seeing that more clearly now.

Ariadne stood up, and we walked back towards the door with trepidation – the rain was still pouring outside, and none of us wanted to go back out into it. We left Bob Owens staring into the flames.

I leant against the cold wall in the hallway, feeling drained, missing the warmth of the fire.

"Now what do we do?" I asked. "We have no idea where Rose is. And someone could be after her. Even if they aren't, anything could have happened to her out there."

"How are we going to find her?" Ariadne wailed.

I really had no idea. Miss Bowler had looked for her and not found anything. How were we supposed to do any better?

"Girls?" Bob was calling us from back in the main chamber. We all turned round and went back to look at him.

"I did see something," he said. "But I didn't think anything of it. One of the rowing boats was missing when I was down there. Now, I know those boats well. I see them every day. I thought someone had just gone out on it, but now I think about it, with the weather... It was the *Skylark*. The *Skylark* was missing."

Scarlet looked at me. "If someone took the boat, then..."

"They might have taken Rose!" Ariadne cried. "We have to find that boat!"

Chapter Thirty-two

SCARLET

We ran back out into the rain, on to the little bridge, this time armed with a pair of Bob's binoculars. Ivy and Ariadne used their arms to form shelter and keep the rain off them, but even then it was hard to see. In fact, everything was a blurry mess.

I fiddled with the focusing knob and soon I could make things out more easily. To the left I could see the hotel and the jetty where we'd rowed from. If they'd taken the boat from there, then surely they must be heading for the other side of the lake. I moved to the right side of the bridge, the others following me, and looked up to the far end. I could make out the biggest of the gushing white waterfalls that fed the lake, and as I looked further, right up to the north... "There!" I said. "I think I can see it!"

"Can I look?" Ivy asked. I handed the binoculars to her and pointed her in the right direction. "I think you're right, that's definitely the boat."

"Come on, let's go!" I hastily returned the binoculars to the inside of Bob's tower and then pulled the enormous door shut behind me. Ariadne was already climbing down into the boat, and I heard the thud as she landed on the wet boards. Ivy was next on the ladder, and then I jumped in behind her. The boat rocked and wobbled, but it stayed afloat.

I missed the warm, dry tower as soon as we'd stepped out, but I was so soaked that I was becoming used to the rain.

This time, Ivy took the oars, and she rowed as fast as she could while we shouted directions. I was distracted by my thoughts as the boat cut through the water – was Bob right? Would the teachers be panicking because we'd gone, or would they be too busy looking for Rose to notice? We had no time to worry about it. They wouldn't be able to find Rose, because they didn't have a clue where to look – and now we did.

It took some time, but as we got nearer to the shore I could see the boat properly. It was definitely the *Skylark*; I could read the peeling paint on the side. It was wedged on the shore like someone had hastily abandoned it. Ivy rowed closer until the boat ground to a halt on the rising pebbles. I hopped out, the cold water splashing on my already-soaked legs, and tied the boat to a nearby tree.

I trudged through the pebbles and peered into the *Skylark*.

"Can you see anything?" Ariadne called out.

There was something black half hidden under the wooden bench. I reached in with both hands and tugged it free, and realised what it was: a helmet.

It was Rose's riding helmet.

Wordlessly, I held it up to the others. Ivy gasped. Rose *had* been in this boat. But with who? And where had they taken her?

Ivy and Ariadne helped each other out of the boat and came over to me. There was another roll of thunder overhead, and we all jumped. I just wished it could all be over, that we could find Rose sheltering somewhere and head back to the hotel and, more importantly, to the warmth of the fireplace. But a sick feeling in my stomach told me that wasn't going to happen.

"Where could she have gone?" Ariadne wailed.

I looked around. There seemed to be a track leading off from the little pebble beach, heading up the hill. But how could we know for sure if Rose had gone that way? She could have gone off into the woods again.

Ivy went over to the track, and I watched as she stared down at the ground. "There's something here," she said. "Footprints!"

There were fresh footprints of different sizes in the mud leading up the track. They were mixed up and hard to make out, but it definitely looked like more than one person had been here. And there were ruts too, like someone had been dragged while resisting.

"This is not good," I said. I turned and started hurrying in the direction the prints led.

Ivy grabbed me. "Scarlet..." she started as I whirled round. "We should turn back and find Miss Bowler. We have no idea who Rose could be with! What if they have a shotgun or something? We can't just go up there alone."

"Are you mad?" I snapped back, shaking her hand away. "There's no time! We need to find her now! And besides, there are three of us! That's hardly alone!"

"But what if—"

"Every time you say 'what if' is another moment we could be saving Rose!" I couldn't believe my sister sometimes.

Ariadne put her arm on my shoulder. "Ivy's right that we

ought to be careful. If we go running up there like headless chickens, we could do more harm than good."

She had a point. "Fine," I said begrudgingly. "But we still need to hurry. We'll just do it *carefully*."

The track led to a set of steps that were little more than rocks jutting out of the hill, slick with rain. We scrambled up them, trying our best to avoid making any noise. It was hard, but if we didn't talk then at least the storm would drown us out.

We emerged through some trees into a barren, muddy clearing. I looked out in horror at the scene.

Rose. She was standing on the edge of the cliff, crying, the wind whipping at her hair.

And there were two figures advancing on her. Figures I recognised.

They were Phyllis and Julian Moss.

I couldn't believe my eyes. I know, people say that all the time, but I really couldn't. I blinked a few times, suspecting that my eyes were lying to me. But each time I opened them, Phyllis and Julian were still there, moving threateningly towards Rose.

The *Skylark*, I realised. Of course that was the boat Julian would choose!

I pulled Ivy and Ariadne behind a rock. Rose was right on the cliff edge. If we jumped out now, something could go badly wrong.

"It's really very simple," Julian said, his voice raised to be heard over the wind and the rain. He sounded nothing like the mild-mannered birdwatcher I'd believed him to be. "You give us the locket, and you can go back to your friends safe and sound. If you refuse, well... you're crazy, aren't you? There's no telling what a crazy girl might do. What if she tragically threw herself in the lake?"

"Do what he says, Rose," Phyllis called. "Then nobody will have to get hurt."

Rose was just shaking her head over and over, terror in her wide eyes. I was terrified that she would lose her footing and fall straight off the cliff. I willed her to stay put with all my might.

"You can't even find the words now, dear cousin?" Julian spread his arms out wide. "You see? You're not right. You're broken. That's what we've been telling you all along."

"*Cousin?*" Ivy whispered.

A horrible feeling began to grow inside me. I remembered what Rose had told us back in our room the other day. About the people in her family who didn't want her to get her inheritance, the very people who had had her locked up in the asylum. And I realised, the nasty ball of guilt growing bigger and bigger, that this was exactly what Violet told us last year. And I hadn't believed her.

"Julian, please," Phyllis said to her husband. "Rose, just tell us where your necklace is. You know it's the right thing to do. We'll look after the estate, I promise."

Ariadne leant forward. *"They don't know where it is!"* she mouthed. They might have guessed Rose wore it, but they'd never seen it.

Julian ignored his wife and carried on yelling into the rain. "We know where the safety deposit box is kept! All we need is the key. We went to a lot of effort to find out that your mother kept it in her locket, you know, not to mention to find out that you were here. We had to do some *persuading*."

I didn't like the sound of that one bit. I was shaking with anger now. How dare these people do this? Who did they think they were?

Rose said something, then, but I couldn't hear it.

"What was that?" Julian cupped a hand to his ear dramatically. "Speak up! Are you making your choice? Give us the necklace, or..." He pointed at Lake Seren, cold and grey and majestic behind her.

Her mouth opened again, but no sound came out. She turned and looked out at the lake.

"Oh no," I whispered. Was she considering jumping? It

was too high, I knew that much. She'd never make it. She'd be seriously hurt, even if she didn't die. And who knew what was under these cliffs? There could be sharp rocks lurking beneath the surface of the water. "Oh God, Rose, don't do it..."

I couldn't let it end like this. Nobody deserved that, and especially not Rose. She didn't deserve to fling herself into the lake believing that nobody cared, that everyone thought she was a freak. I had to do something.

And that was when I made a stupid decision.

"Stay hidden from him," I said to Ivy and Ariadne. "Promise me."

They blinked at me, nodding, before they'd even realised what I was going to do.

"HEY!" I shouted. I jumped up from behind the rock and ran forward, right in front of Phyllis and Julian.

Rose gasped through her sobs.

I raised my fists, ready to fight. "Don't you dare touch her!"

Phyllis and Julian looked shocked for a moment, but then a nasty smile spread across Julian's face. He stepped up close to me. I realised, then, how much taller and stronger than me he was. What had I done?

"You," he said. "I told you to stay out of trouble, didn't I?"

I glared at him. "I prefer to go looking for it. Let Rose go, or I'll..."

"Or you'll what?" he laughed. "We don't need you."

And he reached out and shoved me, and I hit the ground rolling...

And slipped right off the cliff edge.

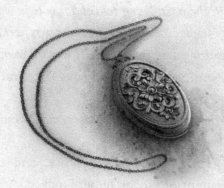

Chapter Thirty-three

IVY

"SCARLET!" I screamed.

My world shattered into pieces.

I think I passed out, just for a second. I hit my head on the rock, and I could feel a cut there, and I knew it was bleeding. But it meant nothing to me. Everything was dull, lifeless.

I couldn't breathe. I couldn't move. Ariadne was shaking me, saying something, but it wasn't hitting my ears. My eyes were squeezed shut.

I was back in the past, being told that my twin was dead. Listening to my stepmother telling me there was nothing they could do. I was drowning in the rain. It was all over.

"Ivy, Ivy, please," Ariadne was crying. The wind howled around us.

And then I heard something that snapped me out of it. Something I'd never heard before.

"HOW COULD YOU?" It was Rose, and she was shouting. Screaming at the top of her lungs.

Slowly, I opened my eyes. My chest hurt. Everything hurt.

Phyllis was tugging on Julian's coat, her face drawn with horror. "No, no, no, this wasn't how it was supposed to go. Julian..."

"Look what you made me do!" Julian whirled round. "If you'd just given me the—"

"SHUT UP!" Rose screamed. "Just shut up!" She put her hand inside her jumper and ripped the necklace from her throat. Julian visibly flinched. Rose shot out her hand and dangled the locket at arm's length, over the lake. "I have..." she gasped, panting, like she wasn't quite sure how to get the words out. "I have carried this key my whole life. Fitzwarren Manor is mine by right. My... my mother hated you, and with good reason! She called you a vulture!"

"Now she speaks!" Julian said, throwing his hands up, but Rose loosened her grip and he choked into silence.

"I am Lady Rose Fitzwarren!" she shouted into the wind. "And I would rather that NOBODY had the family fortune than see a MONSTER like you take one penny of it!"

I watched, cold and numb and sick, as Rose gripped the locket tightly in her hand, and pulled her arm back.

"NO!" Julian roared, running towards Rose, reaching for the locket. But Rose threw with all her might, and the locket arced through the air.

And Julian tumbled after it.

I heard a distant splash from far below.

And I realised something, but hardly dared to think it at that moment – I hadn't heard a splash when Scarlet had fallen...

Phyllis let out a wail of anguish that was unlike anything I'd ever heard, and fell to her knees.

With Julian gone, I got up and ran forward, not knowing what was powering my legs, knowing only that I had to look. I threw myself on the ground and crawled to the cliff edge. "Scarlet!" I called out.

"*Ivy!*"

It was Scarlet. She was hanging on to the cliff.

The colour flooded back into the world.

"Oh, thank God," I sobbed.

"Help me!" Scarlet yelled. She was clinging on by her

fingertips a little below the cliff edge, her feet just balancing on a tiny rocky outcrop.

Seconds later, Ariadne and Rose were beside me.

"Pull her up!"

I reached down, and clamped my hand round Scarlet's right wrist. Rose and Ariadne took the left.

"I don't want to let go!" said Scarlet, tears in her eyes.

"We've got you!" I nodded at the others.

"On three!" Ariadne said. "One... two... three!"

Scarlet let go. We pulled as hard as we could, and she scrambled up over the edge as we all fell backwards, her knees scraping on the rock.

We all lay there for a moment, in a wet heap, not quite believing any of what had just happened. And then Rose pulled Scarlet into a tight hug, and we all joined in. I felt relief like I had never felt before. Scarlet was safe. We were safe.

"He's gone," Rose sobbed. "He's gone."

"It's OK now," Ariadne said. "We've got you."

"I thought I'd lost you again," I said to Scarlet as I hugged her, tears streaming down my cheeks.

"You can't lose me that easily," she said, hugging me back. "We're a team, remember? A team that can't be broken."

* * *

Phyllis was in hysterics, crying and screaming. Scarlet, who had stood up and brushed herself off, grazed knees and all, limped over to her. "Oh, stop that," she said. "This is mostly your fault, you know."

I followed Scarlet over. Phyllis's blonde hair was wild, her eyes red. Her trousers were covered in mud and she was shaking. She looked up at Scarlet. "Julian..." she wailed.

"Who are you really?" Scarlet demanded breathlessly. "Is Phyllis Moss even your real name?"

Phyllis gulped in the cold air. The rain was starting to ease off a little, I thought. "Phyllis Fitzwarren," she said sadly.

Rose and Ariadne came and stood beside us. "You're his new wife," Rose said, just loud enough to be heard. "That's why I hadn't seen you before."

Phyllis nodded, staring out at the lake, not saying a word.

"And you planned all this?" I asked shakily. I was still having trouble coming to terms with the fact that the nice orienteering instructor and her birdwatching husband had been out to get us this whole time.

"I..." Phyllis gulped. "I was just trying to help him, to..." she gave another gasping sob, "to get him what he wanted..."

Scarlet grabbed her arm and pulled her up, and Ariadne took her other arm to stop her running away. "Come on," Scarlet said. "We're going back to the hotel."

I held on to my sister's hand as tightly as I could while we walked down the hill. I wasn't letting her get away again. Not after I'd only just got her back!

As the storm quietened down, we rowed across the lake, Phyllis sitting silently at one end of the boat. Ariadne was still holding on to her in case she tried to escape, but she didn't look like she was going to.

There was no sign at all of Julian. I wondered what had happened to him. Had he drowned, joining the lost souls at the bottom of the lake? It made me feel nauseous to think about it. I hoped he wouldn't come back, but I wasn't sure I wanted him to be dead.

I didn't know what Phyllis believed had happened to him. She wouldn't say a word, her blonde hair sticking to her face as she stared blankly out at the water.

Rose, on the other hand, was unusually talkative. Her voice had gone back to being quiet as a mouse's, and we still strained to hear her over the last of the rain, but there was a fierce determination that I didn't think had ever been there before.

"It was him," she said. "He had me locked up. Since..."

she choked a little on her words. "Since I lost my parents, I'm the sole heir to the Fitzwarren estate and the family fortune. Julian wanted to take it all for himself. When I came to Rookwood, I thought I'd escaped him, so long as I didn't tell anyone who I really was."

We stayed quiet, and listened.

"Nobody ever wanted me." Rose held her head down, the last of the rain dripping from her golden hair. "They all thought I was a freak. That I was mad or cursed. I... I think I believed them." She paused again, then looked up at the rest of us. "Thank you for believing in me."

"Rose... I..." I felt I needed to say this, but it was hard. "We had doubts. The sleepwalking and everything, it was all so unusual."

She bit her lip. "It's all right," she said. "You saved me in the end."

"It's not all right," I said, determined to make up for it. "We're your friends and we should've trusted you, and not let what everyone else said get to us just because things were... well, unusual. I'm sorry."

"We're sorry," I heard Scarlet and Ariadne echo, and I knew they meant it.

"We're all a bit unusual though, aren't we?" Scarlet said as she heaved the oars back and forth. "I was locked up in the asylum too, because I couldn't stay out of trouble.

Everyone thought I was dead. Ivy spent weeks pretending to be me."

"I once burned down a shed!" Ariadne piped up.

"There, you see?" Scarlet said. "You're not alone, Rose. We can all be freaks together."

And for the first time that afternoon, Rose began to smile.

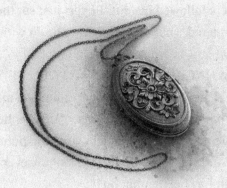

Chapter Thirty-four

SCARLET

I stopped the *Adventure* next to the jetty, and threw the rope over one of the wooden poles. For a moment, I sat back and just felt glad to be alive. I had come close to death so many times now. How many chances did I have left?

I stood up and climbed out of the boat. The rain was turning to drizzle that was fading to mist, and I could feel the sun starting to peek through the clouds. I heard the roar of the dam as it let the water out of the lake.

As the others followed me out, Phyllis just sat there, still staring. I wondered what we were going to do with her.

That was when I heard someone shouting.

"GIRLS! WHAT ARE YOU DOING? GIRLS!"

To no one's surprise, Miss Bowler pounded into view, huffing and panting in her raincoat. "Where have you been!?" she demanded. She looked over and spotted Rose and Phyllis. "And you two! We've been looking everywhere! What on earth has been going on?"

I looked at my friends. "Um," I said. "That's a bit of a long story, Miss..."

We did our best to explain on the way back up to the hotel, Miss Bowler marching Phyllis along after we'd told her exactly what the orienteering instructor had really been up to.

"The police will be coming for you, young madam," she'd chastised, as if Phyllis was one of her students. Phyllis still didn't say a word. She seemed to have given up.

Although Miss Bowler had been furious at us for going out during the storm, she seemed more relieved that it was all over. I was sure Rookwood had had more than enough bad publicity as it was, without losing pupils on the school trip.

We finally made it to the hotel, and we all sat gratefully

in the reception area while Miss Bowler got Mr Rudge to send for the police. The police in this case apparently consisted of two constables who lived in the village over the hill, and Mr Rudge had ordered a kitchen boy to ride over and find them. At least the storm had finally stopped.

After some time and a lot of shouting, Mrs Knight came out from the room where she'd been resting. She looked a good deal better, with her arm in a sling. "Oh, girls," she said when she saw us sitting there. "What *have* you been up to this time?"

I started to explain, but she held up her hand.

"Miss Bowler has already been telling me, but I'm not sure I can quite believe it. In fact, I may need to sit down again." Right on cue, she collapsed into the armchair in one corner. "Julian seemed like such a *lovely* man." She sighed, and her cheeks flushed red again. "I think I've had enough excitement for one trip."

Mrs Knight called for the doctor with the walrus moustache, who cleaned up the cut on Ivy's forehead while she winced, and looked at my bruised and scraped limbs. He declared I was fine, if a little battered.

The evening drew in, and the constables from the village arrived on horseback with the harassed-looking kitchen boy. They told us they had set people to work moving the fallen tree, then wasted no time in getting Phyllis to spill her guts about everything that had happened.

She kept repeating that she was just doing what Julian wanted. I didn't know what she was thinking. No man was worth all that.

Apparently, Julian had concocted a plan to have Rose locked away in the asylum, knowing that, as next in line, he would then become the heir to the fortune. But there was a flaw in his plan – he'd recently heard that, shortly before their deaths, Rose's parents had written a new will cutting Julian out of any inheritance. Rose was the sole heir, and if anything were to happen to her everything would go to charity rather than to any of the other relatives. The new will was secured in their safety deposit box, and only Rose had the key. The key that was now at the bottom of the lake. Julian had been spitting with fury when he'd heard about the new will, and he'd decided his only shot was to make sure that it was destroyed.

He'd apparently caused a scene at the asylum when they had admitted that they'd lost Rose, but he'd learnt that she'd been close to Violet. That had led him and Phyllis to investigate Rookwood, and they'd read about the school trip from Mrs Knight's announcement in the local paper. They'd been stalking us ever since.

I realised, then, how close they'd been to us this whole

time. Following us in the bus, hiding out in the bushes, combing through our room at night after setting off the fire alarm. All this to get Rose's necklace. It was all so clever and so stupid at the same time. And now the police were going to take Phyllis away, and who knew what fate Julian had met.

And much to my surprise, the police weren't the only people who arrived. Later that night, once we were mostly dry and had been given a blissful roast dinner (I wasn't looking forward to returning to stew), there was a commotion in the reception area. We headed over there to find Bob Owens, his hat in his hands, talking to the Rudges.

We'd talked about showing them Ariadne's photographs, but we couldn't believe that he'd actually decided to come clean on his own.

"It was you?" Mrs Rudge said, her hand over her heart.

"Yes, ma'am," he said.

Mr Rudge had gone almost purple. "How dare you? This is our home, and our business! How dare you try to scare us?"

We stepped in between them. I waved at Bob, hoping he would continue.

"I..." He ran a hand through his grey hair. "I'm sorry. I thought it would make up for what happened to my family, see. To my village. But it didn't..."

"That's no excuse! I'm going to tell the constables about

this right away—" Mr Rudge started, but his wife grabbed his arm.

"Oh, stop it, Gerald," she said. "I want to hear what Mr Owens has to say."

So they stood, and listened, Mrs Rudge keeping a tight hold on her husband, while Bob explained everything, just as he had done to us.

Just to add to the surprises, by the time Bob had finished, it was Mr Rudge who had tears in his eyes. Mrs Rudge just looked a little stunned. "Is all of that true?" she said finally.

Bob nodded. "You have my word. Not that my word means much to you, I know. I am sorry, truly." He turned away from them. "I'll pay you back for the damage. Send the police after me, if you like. I haven't got anything left to lose." He started walking towards the door, but Mrs Rudge ran after him and put a hand on his shoulder.

"Mr Owens... Bob... We didn't realise any of that. I'd heard stories about the place being haunted, and I knew about the village, but that was as much as I knew. That's why I was so scared by it all. We shouldn't have tried to cover it up, but I just didn't want to lose all our guests." She looked down at the carpet, ashamed. "I'm sure there's something we could do to help you." She looked back at her husband, who just sniffed and wiped his eyes, and then back at Mr Owens. "Would you like a job?"

"What?" Bob said, along with all the rest of us who were standing in the doorway.

For the first time, I actually saw Mr Rudge smile, and then Mrs Rudge's uncertainty faded away. She wanted to do this. "You know the local area better than anybody. Why don't you work as a tour guide for us?"

Bob couldn't seem to meet her eyes. "I don't know," he said quietly. "I don't know if I should..."

"And we'll do something for your family," she said. "We'll build a memorial for them, and we'll put up a museum about the village. So that people won't forget. Their ghosts can be laid to rest."

"You'd do that?" he asked, his eyes brightening. "For me?"

"Come into the office," she said, "and we'll talk about it."

So we watched as Bob Owens followed the Rudges into their office. Perhaps he was about to find his peace. With Phyllis and Julian gone, I hoped we were about to find ours too.

Chapter Thirty-five

Ivy

The next day dawned bright and hot, which was just another of the unexpected things that happened on the trip. It was as if the sky had rained all it could, and now it was trying something completely different.

The hotel, too, seemed to have changed. It was lighter somehow. Like it was breathing a sigh of relief. I woke up in the four-poster bed and stretched, looking through the tattered curtains at the lake. There were still some silvery clouds, but the sky was blue behind them, and the sun was shimmering on the water.

And then there was Rose. Without her locket, she seemed lighter too. I wondered how she felt, now that her destiny was in her own hands. What would be next for her?

We walked down to breakfast, where we saw Mrs Rudge bustling between the tables with a wide smile on her face. Mr Rudge and Bob had apparently been helping the local men to cut up and move the tree that had fallen over the road. I hoped it might be the start of a friendship between them. Bob certainly needed it.

We were enjoying our food when Elsie and Cassandra walked up to us.

"Oh no," Scarlet said, rolling her eyes. I braced myself.

Elsie was looking at the floor. "Um," she said.

"Um," said Cassandra.

"What's the matter?" Rose asked quietly. "Cat got your tongue?" She had a mischievous smile on her face.

Elsie and Cassandra went bright red.

"MissBowlersayswehavetoapologise," Elsie said in one mouthful.

"What was that?" Scarlet asked, putting her hand to her ear.

"*Miss Bowler says we have to apologise!*" she repeated. "So we're sorry, all right?"

I looked at Rose. "Is that all right with you, Lady Rose?"

Rose made a show of thinking about it, and then she slowly nodded.

"*And?*" Ariadne prompted, twirling her hand around.

"And we were wrong about you and the necklace," Cassandra said. It looked like saying the words physically pained her. "And I shouldn't have accused you of stealing it."

Rose nodded again, that mischievous smile totally priceless.

"I think she'll let you off... *this time*," I said.

"You may go now," Scarlet said, waving them away.

We all collapsed laughing.

Back in our room, we packed up our things. The bus would be able to get through, Mrs Knight had said, now that the tree was cleared. So it was back to Rookwood once again.

In a way, I'd miss this place, I thought as I folded my clothes back into my suitcase. I was glad the trip was over, after all that had happened, but, well... Lake Seren was beautiful, and Rookwood was Rookwood. It was stew and chilly baths and hospital bedsheets. It was the screaming morning bell and chalk dust and endless dark corridors.

But there was something about Rookwood too. With my friends by my side, it wasn't all bad. There were things to be learnt and secrets to uncover.

And besides, we just had to last the rest of the term. Then

it would be time for the summer holidays, and just maybe we'd be allowed to stay with Aunt Phoebe and Aunt Sara. It all depended on whether our stepmother was involved – I just hoped she wouldn't find out about the trip. The last thing we needed was more trouble.

And after the summer? A whole new year at Rookwood. A fresh start, perhaps. Without the shadow of Miss Fox and Mr Bartholomew hanging over everything. Maybe things could really be different this time.

Ariadne placed her final suitcase on top of her stack of them. "Phew," she said, blowing a lock of hair out of her eyes. "I think I'm done!"

"I think you forgot something," Scarlet said.

Ariadne looked distraught. "Oh no! What did I forget?"

"ME!" Scarlet yelled, tackling Ariadne to the floor.

Rose snorted with laughter, and I couldn't help grinning. I couldn't ever forget Scarlet. I had to remember what we'd said – as long as we were together, everything would be all right in the end.

We said our goodbyes to the Rudges, to the hotel guests and to Bob. Scarlet made him promise to behave, and he just laughed and put his hat on her head. Mr Rudge had already begun the plans for the village memorial. Things were changing, moving forward.

Ariadne took one last photograph of all of us together, standing in front of the hotel, in the sun. I had a suspicion that this would be the one to make it into the school newsletter. Well – at least, if she'd managed to avoid the moment where Scarlet was pulling a face.

"I'm going to send this one to Daddy too," Ariadne said as she lowered the camera. "I hope he liked my picture with the water nymphs."

"It was a masterpiece," Scarlet said. "And it cannot be repeated."

Ariadne laughed. "Oh, I don't know," she replied. "I've got some ideas..."

The bus was waiting down the hill, and we all trekked towards it, lugging our suitcases. Mrs Knight counted us on with her good arm, the other still bandaged.

"Can't we just leave those two behind?" Scarlet asked, tilting her head at Elsie and Cassandra.

"Get on the bus, Grey," Miss Bowler said, unimpressed.

You could hear the rush of the dam as we climbed on, still letting out the water from the lake. You could see the surface was getting lower, creeping away from the shoreline.

When Mrs Knight was satisfied that no one had been lost this time, she told the driver to get going. "Right, everyone!" she called out. "Back to Rookwood. After this term, we'll be having a new start. Many new pupils will be joining us..." She took a deep breath. "So let's get this year over with, shall we?" She sat down heavily at the front, with a huge sigh of relief.

I didn't blame her one bit.

The bus began to chug away down the hill, and we took the opportunity to look out over the lake, Scarlet leaning over me, Ariadne and Rose in the seats behind us. It was breathtaking in the sun. Deep blues and greens, the dotted white shapes of sheep on the hills, the fairy-tale tower tall and majestic. It all shone in a valley so beautiful that I could see why Mr Owens loved it so much. The darkness had lifted. I hoped that the spirits of the villagers might rest now.

"Oh my gosh!" Ariadne said suddenly. "Look!"

I peered out, and realised what she was pointing at. Everyone gasped, and Ariadne – of course – took a photograph.

There, in the lake, I could see the tip of the church tower rising from the waters. I wondered, as the breeze blew, if the bells might start to ring.

"Goodbye, Lake Seren!" Scarlet waved as we drove past. "Goodbye, Shady Pines!"

But I was still staring at the church tower.

And I could have sworn, for a moment, that I saw something golden glinting in the sunlight.

THE END

Acknowledgements

This book owes a debt to my own school trips, where we stumbled over sheep skulls in muddy forests, listened to ghost stories in pitch-black caves and climbed jutting cliffs in the rain. And also to my parents, for taking me to visit the stunning Lake Vyrnwy, one of the places on which this book is very loosely based.

There are many more people who have helped bring this book to life. Thanks go to:

My marvellous editors – Lizzie Clifford for all her support with the series and in helping to plan this book, and Sarah Hughes and Samantha Stewart for lending their editing expertise in the later stages. And to all the fab folk at HarperCollins, who have worked so hard.

Superagent Jenny Savill, and all at Andrew Nurnberg Associates.

Illustrators Kate Forrester and Manuel Šumberac – thank you for interpreting my words so beautifully. And to Elisabetta Barbazza, who is a fantastic cover designer.

My indispensable writing-advice givers: r/YAwriters, #UKMGchat, the Bath Spa gang and the MA Writing Group of Wonders. I don't know where I'd be without all of you lot!

To my online followers, and to those who spend time chatting with me or counselling me – you are wonderful; please don't change.

Last but never least, to Ed, and to all my friends and family. Thank you for existing. You are my favourites.

And, as always, thank *you* for reading. I hope you enjoyed the trip, but soon we'll be returning to Rookwood, and All Hallows' Eve is approaching...